WARRIORS AND LOVERS

WARRIORS AND LOVERS

True Homosexual Military Stories

Volume 2

Edited by Winston Leyland

Leyland Publications
San Francisco

ACKNOWLEDGMENTS
The following William Cozad stories were first published in the following magazines: "Soldier Boy" (*Torso*, June 1988); "Cadet Commander" (*Inches*, Aug. 1991); "Soldier" (*Inches*, Dec. 1991); "Valentine Sailor" (*Torso*, March 1990); "Black-Balled!" (*Stallion*, Jan. 1991); "The French Sailor" (*Stallion*, Aug. 1989); "Night Bus to Reno" (*Inches*, Dec. 1990); "Flyboy" (*Stallion*, May 1989); "Sailor's Surprise" (*Male Insider*, March 1991).

ISBN 0-943595-37-1

Leyland Publications
P.O. Box 410690
San Francisco, CA 94141
Complete catalog of available books is $1.00 postpaid.

CONTENTS

INVITATION TO OUR READERS

If you've read and enjoyed this book, *Warriors and Lovers*, or our earlier volume in this series, we invite you to write about some past sexual experience that is vivid in your mind, whether from your young manhood, or from last week, e.g., my first college homosexual experience, sex encounters when a soldier/sailor, etc. But no under legal age experiences, please. All material should be based on true experiences — no fiction or fantasies. Manuscripts submitted should be typed, double spaced, from 5 to 25 pages. If your manuscript is accepted, it will be published in a future book either anonymously or with your name as byline (whichever you request). We regretfully cannot return any manuscripts, but you will receive free copies of the volume in which your work appears. Please send material to: Leyland Publications, P.O. Box 410690, San Francisco, CA 94141.

WARRIORS AND LOVERS

RICK JACKSON

I WASN'T LOOKING for tight, hard marine butt. Shit, when you're deployed for six months on an LST with three hundred other marines and a couple hundred dick-hungry sailors, checking out ass in the shower is the last thing you do. You get really good at stumbling through the day with blinders on, ignoring the packages in the weightroom, the dicks swinging slapping hard marine thighs in berthing, the ballbags handing heavy and low. You have to get good at it. A lot of other guys on the ship want the same things you do, but you also have quirky homophobic assholes around who at least claim they don't want your thick dick up their butts. They probably do, of course, but would eat nails before they'd admit how they really felt. Any young marine who is too friendly finds himself bounced out of the Corps before the shit on his dick is dry. Even in my straight-arrow mode, though, there was no way I could let Bob's bouncy bubble butt slide past with a casual glance. In a real world, the government would have put it into a museum for the public at large to venerate. Don't get me wrong — nearly all marines have good asses. The Corps keeps us humping cross-country enough that we don't have a chance to let our bodies grow slack and lazy the way Navy squids do. Even by marine standards, though, Bob's butt was epic. He didn't have a hint of slack; his great, hard-muscled ass jutted out proudly from his hips as if to tell the world what a good time he was going to be for the first foxy young stud who made a move. It was hairless and tanned and had the rich, soft transient glow of youth. Bob was only eighteen, but most kids his age have lost the supple softness that lingers through infancy and finally dies a slow death in adolescence. Bob's hard marine body was like steel bands tightly coiled within a baby's skin. He was all rippling muscle so soft to the touch that you would almost rather admire than fuck him. Almost.

That day, I lost control of myself. He was turned away from the door so I didn't think he'd notice. My eyes shamelessly raped his hard marine flesh until he turned quickly around and caught me looking at him. I tried to cover with some shit about looking for a towel I'd left behind, but I blushed and stammered and did everything but sink open-mouthed to my knees. Oh, I was smart enough to steer clear of him for awhile, and I might have been OK if I'd scored ashore in Singapore. Our last night in, though, I struck out again for a perfect record: zero for four. It wasn't that I *couldn't* get laid. Asians were all over me. I just wasn't interested. Once you've seen Bob's butt naked, you don't go out and settle for scrawny Asian ass. Getting shit-faced was a mistake. For one thing, it didn't help ease my frustration. For another, it made me even hornier — if that were possible. By the time I got back to the ship, I was in sad shape. I puked in a taxi, barfed on a couple of schoolgirls in the MRT subway car, and up-chucked on the pier — and myself. My idea — to the point I was thinking clearly enough that night even to have an idea — was to shower and fall into my rack to sleep off my desire and frustration along with my drunk. Sure enough, though, some passing god decided to fuck with me first. Bob stood bare-assed, flexing his muscles and admiring himself in the shower when I got there. Everybody else in berthing was either still on the beach or racked out solid.

"Fuck it!" I thought to myself. I tore off my t-shirt and shorts and tossed them into the trash, threw my towel to the deck, and slipped into the shower where Bob was smearing foamy white suds across his beautiful bare backside. He started to look around, but I wasn't in the mood for a fucking conversation. This wasn't about courtship or comradeship or any other fucking ship. This was about getting me laid. Period. I lay my left hand across his strong, tanned shoulders and pushed his face to the wall of the shower. My other hand took over the job of soaping the crack in his butt. I rubbed the slick suds deep between his massive marine manmuscles, spreading those cheeks wide as the hot water coursed down his back and splashed off his ass onto my legs. His butt instinctively began to grind against my hand and, softly at first and then as loudly as he dared, he let moans and whimpers of pleasure ooze up from his soul and escape to mingle with the sizzle of the shower and the splash of the water onto the deck. His butt, soft and hairless and strong, wriggled in my hand like a spastic snake until, almost as though by accident, my fuckfinger slipped into the pucker that bounded his virtue — and my need.

My lips attacked his wet neck and soulders. His body was writhing against the shower wall, so my restraining hand was free to slide across his bootcamp-cut hair and, eventually, to ease down across his massive hairless chest and tweak his hard, passion-tipped tits. I didn't fingerfuck his ass. I didn't have to. He was grinding and thrusting and gyrating so much that his butthole wriggled up my fuckfinger like an inspiration. Through the water, I heard a long, soul-felt "AAAAAAHHHHHHHHH" as my finger slid into the soft pink tightness, and I knew he'd been longing to have me inside him as much as I'd needed to be there. I suddenly felt not only sober, but almost liberated as though the endless chalkboard screek that had been relentlessly gnawing at my soul was suddenly silenced. My spirits unwound like a coiled spring, and I knew that peace was just a soapy butt-fuck away.

I took my time with him. I hadn't been inside another man in three months, but some deep, ancient urging slowed my pace and made me savor each rough caress, the texture of his slick shit-chute along my fuckfinger, the stubble of his hair against my palm, the soft, wet thrill of his shoulder against my lips, the long drawn-out moans of greedy animal pleasure that eased themselves unbidden from his lips. I wanted a good, solid fuck; but I was more than willing to settle for more. My chest slid against his back and I felt his slick, naked flesh slide against my fur-covered chest. For the first time, my nasty little mind turned from his ass to his boy-warrior face. In many ways he was an Alexander: hard and lean and fit for battle, yet blessed with a pug nose and green eyes and enough freckles to decorate a tribe of leprechauns. Bob's body was the beauty of man incarnate — the best of the young, the glory of a hunk in his prime, and, he soon proved beyond question, the perfection of a stud skilled beyond his years.

I wasn't about to stand fecklessly behind him all night with his butt wrapped around my finger. I had something much meatier in mind. My thick nine inches slid between his soapy, marine-muscled mounds and eased against his wrinkled sea-pussy. His tender hole reached out to kiss my lizard, begging me to hurry, calling me like a siren to smash myself into his rock-hard body.

My hands slid across his chest and down his rippled belly, devouring him with every hungry stroke as he slipped in my arms like a mating eel. My lips sucked fiercely at his ear lobe, but, as my tongue darted into his ear as though to fuck my way to his brain, his body convulsed against me, driving his tight manhole up my throbbing crankshaft. He slipped over my purple, passion-pulsing nob in one swift stroke and then lingered for a brief, regretful moment, his wet, naked body dangling off the end of my dick like an impure thought. Then, a second seizure even more violent than the first sent him lunging up my shaft until all nine inches of my joint were imbedded inside his guts. My palms clutched at his nipples, sliding over his wet flesh while those hard passion-tipped tits drilled his passion into my hands as surely as my cock was spreading his ass.

I lay quietly inside him for a moment, considerate and unwilling to break the spell of perfection that had enchanted us both. As the gasps for air that had greeted his impaling slowly gave way to the rapid, shallow breaths reminiscent of the delivery room, I worked my stiff pubes against the ruins of his tight marine butt and ground into him, twisting my cock inside his fucktunnel, shoving my hard dickhead into the nether reaches of his guts, grating my cock slowly across his prostate. His rapid, frenzied pants grew even more erratic as I began a long, slow withdrawal — pulling about eight of those thick nine inches from him. Only my trigger-ridge kept his ass hooked, but lust had swollen me wide and, like some mongrel cur with a bitch, I was his for the duration. My cock slid back down the slickened chute of our union and crashed headlong into the tender tissues of his guts. My hips jolted with a THWACK into his hard jock ass and, almost before that sound could ricochet off the shower walls, I was leaving him again, stroking up and slamming down like a defective piston in a run-away engine. My cadence quickened as the alternating sensations of dick and vacuum, of fulfillment and abandonment, of renewed joy and sorrow came over more quickly. I felt his slick flesh sliding along my meaty monorail like a fucking express to ecstasy. Our bodies landed against each other like battling moose at the rut. Indeed, the harder we did the dirty but glorious deed, the less we felt modern examples of America's fighting finest. The thin veneer of civilization dropped away and left us both jungle savages who took what they wanted, when they wanted, and for as long as they wanted.

My hands slipped to Bob's thighs as I grabbed past his massive marine member and cum-choked loadstones to grasp him from the front and pull him even farther up my raging manmeat and pound his helpless body harder and faster against the shower wall. He slammed back and forth like a rag doll, his muscles and bearing and all that made him a marine overcome by the primitive, delirious need which gripped us both and drove us frantically and irresistibly onward. The hot, steamy water blasted our flesh, but our passions boiled even hotter. The savage instinct of our species drove us faster than any marine cadence until we fucked and thrusted and rammed together, helpless to resist the primeval compulsion that had become our master. Time seemed to skid to a stop as consciousness gave way to instinct and every raw nerve became passion's plaything. The dark mists of ancient lusts blew away the shower and ship and all we had known, leaving only our tangled, naked flesh sliding and grinding together through the eternal void. I held onto Bob's butt, pulling it ever harder up my dick, as though that round pink hole was my salvation, my grail. Every time my hips bashed against that classic ass, every time my cock skewered his guts, Bob let slip a low, almost subsonic grunt of satisfaction. As I locked my teeth into Bob's broad shoulders, consciousness finally faded away entirely. We slipped together into the maelstrom, lost together in the timeless tumult of our terrible ecstasy. I'll never know how many seconds or years we rammed and thrusted and fucked together, helpless to escape the torrent that swirled about us. Eventually, I remember a cry of savage terror or conquest or pain that pierced the veil between that world and this. The cry came closer and louder and, suddenly, I knew it was my own. Almost at once I felt my guts heave as my ballbag contracted and my loadstones blasted their cargo in great, white-hot pulses up through my cum-chute and out through the huge organic fire-hose nozzle I'd parked deep inside Bob's beautiful jock marine butt. As one nut after another racked my body and soul, as my guts turned inside out and flushed through my dick to empty into his, I felt at once the friction that had been long building fade to nothing. The fire we had stoked unknowingly was suddenly slaked and replaced by so smooth a symphony of ecstasy that the very angels of paradise could but have listened in awe. Bob's gurgles of feral satisfaction soon added themselves to mine as he broke free of my clutches, not to escape but to throw himself harder and more fiercely up my plunging cock, demanding that every single whip-tailed little trooper I had join the multitude his greedy, slutty jock marine ass had already sucked from my poor helpless dick. His butt banged into me so hard he knocked me backwards against the far wall of the shower, but still he fucked his tight marine asshole harder up my dick. My body gave a final shiver of primitive satisfaction at a job well done as the last of my cream load of marine spooge oozed out into his ass. I collapsed onto his back, panting like a tormented fiend of hell and simply hung on until he had enough of strangling my lizard with his sphincters and allowed me to escape.

When I'd raped his butt, I'd loosed the genie from the bottle. Now that he'd had a taste of dick, he was ready for Thanksgiving dinner. Even before I was completely free of his hole, he was trying to spin me around to use me as he wanted. He sank to his knees and buried his pug nose up my butt. I'd never been much into rimming, but, then, I'd never felt Bob's anteater tongue up my butt or had that cute little pug nose doing what came naturally. Just then, I was one whipped puppy, but the bastard wasn't about to give me a chance to catch my breath. That nose slid along the hairy crack of my ass like Patton through Germany. When it hit home, his tongue took over and drilled deep while that innocent little pug nose shuddered from side to side to keep my own well-muscled ass from closing in. Bob wasn't just a tongue-fucker; he was an artist. The tip of his tongue attacked my fuckhole like a swarm of starving locusts, dancing around the rim, gliding between the folds of my twitching pucker, and pounding into the pit to pull the goody he craved from my depths. For the first half second, I was grossed out; but after that, I was mesmerized. His tongue might as well have been connected to Hoover Dam. Every flick and stroke and slice of his tongue tip at once jolted me to the core and slipped me deeper into my lust-struck trance. I could have stood there with my legs apart, that boyish face up my butt, forever while his mouthorgan played one symphony after another. Subconsciously petting the back of his head as though he were a puppy, I remember being surprised at how soft his hair was. It was more like a cat's than a man's — but since he was going to be my sea-pussy for the next few months — and, if he's lucky, beyond — I guess that's appropriate. Mainly just then I was trying not to moan so loudly that the whoosh of the water wouldn't drown out the noises of my love-struck pleasure. The last thing I needed just then was a skulk of marines to slink in to join the action. I wanted that tongue all to myself and, fortunately, Bob didn't seem to mind. For a while. Then he decided I should prove my love.

He moved around and shoved the biggest, thickest marine dick I'd ever seen smack into my face. All I could do was gape in ad-miration and, before I knew it, I had something stuck in my throat. I managed to pull him out again so my tongue could do justice to the huge, sloppy foreskin that dangled from the front of his gorgeous dork. My tongue slid between the 'skin and the silky-smooth manmeat that lay hidden below. My lips pulled even more of his 'skin up along his shaft to curl up over my tongue. I found his cum-slit lost under the secret folds of his man-hood and began to slither in and out of his man-gash. The taste of musk melded with sweat and, perhaps, the lingering hint of some carelessly shaken piss drew me south across his hot, hard dickhead. As my mouth watered and spit dropped down into the void between his head and 'skin, I slurped up his musky good-ness like a cocker spaniel, greedy and shamelessly abandoned. My tongue pried out the narrow folds beneath his cock and slithered everywhere, stripping away the manmusk he had so carefully guarded from the world. When I prodded too far and hit his trigger-ridge, the tender canopy ripped back in one swift mo-tion to lay the throbbing, vein-rich secrets of his cocksock open to the relentless pillage of my tongue. His luscious knob slid back to make a home in the tight, tender tissues of my throat as his hips came alive to their lusty destiny and began slamming his marine manmeat farther and deeper down into my face. My hand reached round to grab the same butt I'd lately fucked, but this time going, I was on the receiving end of the dick — and loving every face-slapping, bone-crunching minute.

Young Bob liked ramming his deadly dork down my gullet just fine — for awhile. His moans and grunts and cocky leers of pleasure showed well enough that he thought he was in charge. From there, though, he took about ten seconds to discover that tight as my throat was, I had another hole that would be even more fun. I suppose the studly thing to do would have been for me to give him shit, but when you stop to look at it, turn about *is* fair play. I was all for chugging his spunky load down my facehole, but he wasn't having any. He had his dick set on a good, solid buttfuck, so I got to my feet, turned round, and spread my tight, tender marine ass.

I was ready for him to hurt. Any dick that size would have to; it stands to reason. For the first six or eight seconds, my butt felt like Joan at the stake. The weird thing was how quickly the pain turned to pleasure and torment to ecstasy as though my body had known all along what it craved. Something about the way I was turned on changed everything. Maybe it was the way his hands were fucking with my tits and the way his teeth had locked themselves like a jungle cat's into the back of my neck. Maybe it was the delicious wicked abandon of fucking a brother marine in the shower of a Navy LST. Whatever it was, before his throbbing member was shaft-deep up my tight slutty fuckhole, I was one very happy camper. Every sensation that should have been agony turned to mirrored ecstasy and showed me how much fun being on the other end of the stick could be. Each jolt of his gyrine joint gave me more of a rush than the last. What that devastating dick did to my prostate as it slid and scraped and pounded past I'd never have believed possible. Bob grew all butch and used me like his personal whore — and I ate his fucking treatment with a spoon despite myself. Within five minutes, his torment of my prostate had given me my very first anal orgasm — only the first of many. Once I'd turned him on, there wasn't any stopping the kid and he fucked my butt until I thought we were both goners. By the time I felt his pearly jism jet up my shit-chute, I was ready to slam his ass to mush. We kept at it, fucking and loving and teaching each other the ways of real male love until we were both exhausted and reveille brought more men into the head. They gave us sly looks as we limped out to our racks, but by then, neither of us much gave a fuck. Shit, we couldn't. We were just too fucking sore.

PLATOON SUPPORT

BRAD HENDERSON, USMC

When Marine officers deploy on Navy ships, they share staterooms.
Only the CO and XO [commading and executive officers]
get staterooms of their own — as a rule.

W E'D BEEN FLOATING around the Gulf, waiting to help the
UN teams monitor Iraq, for what seemed six years instead
of only six months. Then my roommate's wife squirreled out. I
never heard the full story because they had been transferred by
the time we got back to Pendleton, but apparently she developed
the habit of wandering around the base grazing off peoples'
lawns. Whether because she wasn't doing a good job of keeping
the grass even or because the Corps thought she needed closer
supervision, battalion got a message ordering my roommate back
stateside. He was on the next flight out of Bahrain, and I was left
in a two-man stateroom all by myself. I could lie in my rack and
milk the bone all night if I wanted to. Life was sweet.

I was an AAV [Amphibious Assault Vehicle] platoon leader, so
my marines were always stopping by with some problem or
other. The combination of the ship's ACs doing fuck-all and the
130° temperatures outside made life aboard uncomfortable
enough for the ship to authorize "tropical uniforms." My marines stroked around in khaki shorts and olive t-shirts to keep
them from becoming heat casualties aboard. The t-shirts were bad
enough, showing every hard ridge of muscle and pointy tit they
had. The shorts were worse: so short huge sweaty marine balls
hung out whenever they sat down. Keeping my mind on business wasn't easy. Somehow my concentration just seemed to
wander from maintenance reports to the cum-clogged young nuts
lying loose in the chair across from me. I would see hard young
thighs and the hairy balls between them, not to mention an occasional dickhead peeking out at me, and suddenly fuel pumps
didn't seem all that important. Jefferson made things even worse.

Lance Corporal William Thomas Jefferson sat across from me
bitching about how Gunny Smith wasn't letting him do this and
try that. Normally, I'd have told the kid not to be a whiner, but

I knew perfectly well that Gunny was a pig-ignorant Georgia dick whose daddy would have done the world a big favor if he'd splashed that particular load into some other hole instead. I also knew that Jefferson had his shit in one sock and that the maintenance routine he was suggesting using on the 'tracks was good to go. None of that much mattered. I'd surrendered to my fate and was having a good time scoping out the huge left nut and fine, uncut dickhead I saw parked between us in his chair. I was about to tell him I'd look into the problem with Gunny, but that since CO was big on not jumping the chain of command, he shouldn't hope for much. I was about to tell him that — when Jefferson must have noticed my own dick start to dance. I didn't want it to, but I hadn't used it on anyone in months. Even marines are human.

Jefferson looked at my lizard and gulped. He gave me a queasy look and then looked at the closed door. Then he gulped again. I was about to say something butch about how only faggots noticed crotches or how much I needed a bitch to bone, but before you could say "Be my boy-bitch, baby!" he'd slipped out of his chair and was between my knees, licking at my thigh and exposed nut, and calling my meat farther out of my shorts as though it were a slightly retarded chipmunk lost in the woods. What could I do? The little bastard was practically raping me. I already felt the tell-tale tickle of pre-cum oozing up and out. In another second my marine would have my joint in his mouth.

I think it's a sign of the times that I was more interested in getting my rod rubbered than I was looking at the ethics of letting one of my marines suck dick. I reached up into the drawer where I kept them waiting for the liberty that never came and threw Jefferson a rubber: "If you're going to suck dick, faggot, do it right."

I lifted my ass far enough off the chair so he could pull my shorts down. My nine thick inches were long since daring to be great. They slammed up against my t-shirt with a meaty thwack and waited for adventure. I sat silent before him, letting Jefferson pull back my foreskin and inhale a lungful of eau de dick. The drop of clear pre-cum that glistened an inch from his nose was obviously twisting at his guts the way a stray puppy works on a boy. He wanted to swallow my unpackaged meat in the worst way, but we both knew we were risking enough as it was. One hand cupped my heavy balls, weighing them like a housewife with a melon; the other crowned my cock with the rubber and slowly forced it down over the head, wantonly smearing my dick-lube around in the process.

Once the roll snapped down onto my shaft, Jeff's eager wet lips kissed the end of my meat and began working lower, unrolling the rest of the rubber along my rod as he went. The way his lips slipped and slid across my throbbing joint guaranteed the horny cocksucker didn't lack motivation, but just in case, my hand on the back of his cute little head of black curls helped screw his hole on down my pole. The Marine Corps didn't call Jefferson a lance corporal for nothing. The slut had definitely done this before. By the time my head was ramming into the back of his, those wet lips were stretched around the base of my bone, nipping at my pubes and begging for trouble. His throat was practiced torment, alternately choking on my bone and slip-sliding across my quivering cockhead until every nerve seemed at once ready to erupt, yet stunned into a wetdream of delight. His suction and the little bobs of his cute marine face up and down my dork dug me deeper and deeper down his fox hole.

I wasn't about to just sit there and watch one of my marines suck dick. I reached down, stripped off his shorts, and lifted his body upward as I fell backwards into my rack. The horn-dog didn't miss a beat. My head landed in his crotch, the finest landing zone this marine had ever seen. I wriggled out of my t-shirt and lifted his so I could look up to see his flat, bare belly, knotted by marine-built muscle.

I couldn't resist playing with his 'skin. We uncut men come across our own kind so rarely that the joy of sliding someone else's 'skin up and down across a smooth, purple, plum-sized knob and smelling the savory scent of a natural man is hard to resist. I played with Jeff's cocksock, gooey with his own pre-cum, until I knew I had to cloak his cock before I gobbled him for fucking lunch.

I didn't slip his latexed lizard into my mouth immediately, though. The day's sweat had collected in his crotch, distilling a liqueur no cock-sucking connoisseur could pass up. My nose wriggled its selfish way between his neglect-distended ballbag and a pale thigh to let my tongue police his action. His hips slashed instinctively downward, grinding his crotch even harder against my face. My hands naturally fell onto his hard butt and stayed there, digging into the sultry, sweat-soaked swamp of his asscrack. The slut's hips ground between my face and fingers, scraping out every particle of his manmusk until I was delirious with long-forbidden aromas finally force-fed me willy-nilly.

While I was busy with his crotch, my bitch was sucking prime-time dick. Whether because of his tight throat or his serious suction or the cloud of musk enveloping my consciousness or, maybe, all of the above, I suddenly had too much of a good thing. My satyr-sated guts turned inside out and flushed my balls clean in one blast of jarhead jism after another that should have sent my bitch's head into orbit. My legs locked onto his ears and kept him from moving while I used his tight marine mouth the way I'd been using my fist for the last four months. Except my fist isn't as tight or warm — and knows when it's had enough. Jefferson's gullet kept gulping my jism until I was sure I'd blown a nut in more ways than one.

Fortunately Jeff's crotch smothering my face kept my stifled cries of doomed dickstruction from bellowing out loudly enough to be heard over the whir of the ventilator fans in the next staterooms. I finally gobbled Jefferson's joint, fully intending to show him that an officer and a gentleman could suck dick as well as any 'trackie boot lance corporal. That boot fit too snugly around my crank to let go, though. I wriggled and jiggled and tried to shake myself out of his throat, but Jefferson, having finally found a dick to suck, was determined not to let it get away. Taking a bone away from Cujo would have been easier, but I knew my marine weapon couldn't stand much more abuse. On the other hand, initiative *does* deserve to be rewarded.

I rolled Jefferson's cocksucking body off me and grabbed a fistful of the black curls atop his head to jerk his jarhead back and up off my knob. When I'd recovered what was mine, my load was still safely wrapped, but rapidly trickling its sweet, creamy way down my dick to leak out across my balls. For what I had in mind, a new rubber was certainly called for. While my marine used cock-deprivation as an excuse to gulp in some O_2, I changed into a fresh outfit.

Fortunately for Jefferson, I found a lubed model for our next exercise. He lay beside me, still panting and looking at me with his soulful brown eyes, knowing very well what was up — but not what I intended doing with it. I soon clued his ass in: "So you like playing with a man's dick, do you faggot? Like this." About half way through my growl, I'd pulled his ass out of my rack and bent him double so his chest was draped over my washbasin and his butt was where it belonged.

My dick slammed hard up his hungry ass before either of us was really ready. I'd intended to take my time ramming my rod through the gates of his doubtful but very savory virtue. His butt battered backwards up my bone, propelled by the simple cock-craving instinct of a young grunt on a float. Once he had me where he wanted me, though, he discovered I was too much of a great thing and bounced forward, fast as a sprinter out of the starting blocks. He might even have had momentum enough to make it off the swollen end of my joint if the washbasin hadn't been in the way. As it was, his pelvis lay trapped between the cold porcelain and my hot hips.

I let my plow lie idle for a moment so his furrow could gauge the temper of my steel and the bite in my blade before I began to harrow his ass the way it begged to be tilled. We both knew I was ready to sow more seed; and, as my lips slipped across the gooseflesh on his shoulders and neck to find his ear, we both knew that when my bountiful harvest came in, young Jefferson would feel his ass had been reaped shitless by the jolly Jackson giant.

His sweaty back ground into the wiry red thatch that lives across my chest and belly. My lips sucked at his ear lobes and brought one shiver after another bubbling up from some well-spring of sensibility normally off-limits to his stoic marine nature. My eyes slipped past his high cheekbones to find our image graven in the mirror above my washbasin. I'd alway gotten off watching myself in mirrors or on videotape as I did men hard and long, but there was something so elemental about the haunted, hungry look in Jefferson's eyes that even I was momentarily embarrassed. His lips were parted in pleasure as he ground against my body, writhing in sensuous appreciation as my puissant power seized absolute control over his flesh and dominion over his soul. His whoresome hands reached back to cup my ass and pull me harder up his butt. As I watched his face in the mirror and felt his scabbard quiver on the end of my sword, his eyes rolled back in his head and the hint of hunger I had noticed quickly disappeared into a mist of almost monstrous rapture.

My hands pinched his hard tits; my forearms pressed tight against his flanks to hold him fast while I slammed him faster up the ass. I'm normally a careful, gentle lover; but I'd been denied too long. Once I slid into motion, I bounced my tight 20-year-old lance corporal butt off the unyielding porcelain like a thing possessed. That's how I saw him just then: no longer a member of my platoon, but a thing to be possessed, to be done hard up the butt and discarded after it was broken open and no longer tight enough to slash any more satisfaction out of my reaming, pounding, butt-busting marine pride and joy. I stroked and slammed up his ass, feeling him trying to escape and not caring. My hands at his tits pulled him backward, hard against my cruel cock even as my hips bounced him forward. Both of us stifled our grunts of painful pleasure and baleful whimpers of bliss until, just before the end came and I joined it.

A momentary trance of unreality gripped what was left of my consciousness as surely as my hands had locked onto Jeff's swollen tits. We were both screaming savage ecstasy to the heavens with our souls, yet were coupling like speechless specters, made muter than any mime by the priggish fear others would hear our struggle with the beasts within us and interfere. One glorious primitive sensation merged silently with the next until they became a blend of surreal unreality and sublime expressionism on the grandest human scale.

After an age, I recovered my humanity to find my thick bone drained of its marrow, yet still grinding into the depths of my lanced corporal's remains. My teeth lay locked hard into his neck in jungle celebration of our rutting rite; my lungs threatened ready to explode for lack of air. I opened my eyes again to find gratitude and slavish worship reflecting out of the mirror. Drained and content, I freed his tits and neck and, slowly forced my bone to surrender his flesh — for the time being.

When I turned his ass around to give him a kiss and the comradely marine hug he had earned, I discovered that while I'd been up his butt, Jefferson had been a very naughty young marine. His dick was still hard enough to fuck a first lieutenant, but his rubber was awash with creamy enlisted jism. I don't think Jefferson expected I'd put out, but seeing him hump my hole was such a rush that I didn't mind his being a pain in the ass. Toward the end, when his gungy marine meat was drilling away up my ass, the kid found such a goofy, radiant expression to wear, I'd have adopted him on the spot. A moment later, the demons that live within every man ripped away the cherub's mask and left only the torment of limitless ecstasy behind for me to ponder. When he collapsed into my arms, a sweaty mass of panting marine pride, we both knew that afternoon was just the first of many conferences we'd be having during the rest of the float. As he dragged his load out of my ass and stripped and cleaned his weapon, I had an even more sobering thought: once the word got out I had a single room, Jefferson was just one of the marines in my platoon who would be coming to call.

BLOWJOB ON THE ORIENT EXPRESS

M EN IN YUGOSLAVIA are drafted for two years of compulsory military service in the year when they turn 18. These teenagers are purposefully stationed in barracks far from their home towns, and normally they travel there by train. It is the custom to make a big party in honor of the draftee all night before he is to enter the army, and then to see him to the train station the next day still drinking and singing sentimental and patriotic songs. As a result, the main street leading to the train station in any large Yugoslav town is the scene of high spirited processions of men swigging beer and singing loudly virtually every day during the summer. The youths are permitted to visit their homes for brief periods, and these same towns will be filled with nubile young men in crew cuts and khaki uniforms.

Since my work used to involve traveling by train through Yugoslavia in the summer, I have shared compartments with these drunken teenage boys more than once. In the north of the country, you sometimes see blond beauties reminiscent of the best German or Polish types, but more often the Yugoslav teenager tends toward those dark Balkan good looks that age rapidly but are exquisite in their prime. His swarthy skin is often smooth or lightly bearded with silky dark hair. His frame is tall and loose, his bones large, the jaw square and prominent, the cock uncircumcised, unless he is a Moslem.

It is a hot August afternoon. I am riding the Orient Express south from Belgrade and find myself the only foreigner in a car full of seven young Serbian and Bosnian soldiers getting drunk and singing long, slow, loud, mournful songs as they head to their respective units. The crowded compartment reeks of tobacco, plum brandy, garlic, and young male sweat. I am seated next to the window, facing south as the train heads for Macedonia. The hot sun beats into the cabin, and the heated breeze from the open window seems to emphasize rather than counteract the raunchy atmosphere. I look at the slender young soldier sitting next to me. He shaves his sideburns and moustache, but long, dark, untouched hairs proclaim his youth. His short hair is as black as a Gypsy's, his skin shines sleek and clear, the color of burnished bronze, smooth as polished walnut, with brown-black eyes. His lips are full and sensuous, teeth sharp, uneven, but sparkling white. He smells of youthful perspiration, not sharp or sour but musky. His name is Goran. He is a Serb from Mostar, the capital of Hercegovina, but is on his way to his unit in Kumanovo.

As we pass the time smoking aromatic Balkan tobacco, eating white cheese and grapes, drinking homemade plum brandy, talking about life in America and Yugoslavia, it seems to me that he presses his khaki trousered thigh against me and stares at my crotch. But perhaps it is simply the motion of the train and the fact that we are crowded on the seat; perhaps I am misjudging the direction of his eyes. My elbow touches his dark bare flesh and feels its warmth. He gets up to go to the bathroom and I notice that he is short, about 5'5", with full heavy buttocks. I think about how smooth his gold-bronze ass must be, with pitch black hairs curling darkly out of his pink rosebud virgin asshole. How I want to lick that tender spot of Serbian boy-flesh and thrust my tongue deep into his fragrant warm depths!

Night falls, the compartment darkens. The odor of unwashed feet is added to the fragrances already filling the compartment as the young soldiers take off their black boots to get comfortable for the night. We all sleep sitting up. I lean against the wall and Goran leans slightly against me. I shift slightly so that I am leaning on the deep-breathing soldier boy in that stifling compartment reeking of young Balkan male odors. The rocking motion of the train combined with the effect of the rough plum alcohol have me seething with desire. Fighting to keep from falling asleep in case I get up the courage to make a pass, I suddenly feel his fingers brush my leg and just as suddenly his hand drops onto my thigh. Is it a movement in his sleep or a signal? Heart beating so loudly in my ears that I can barely move my shaking right hand, I place it on his and gently move it across and towards his thigh. Very slowly I begin to touch his upper thigh, trying to feel if he is hard or not. He has a raging boner! His response is quick but subtle as he slides his hand into my hardening crotch in the dark, stinking compartment full of snoring soldiers.

I am overwhelmed by the reality of what I am experiencing. I actually have my hand on a teenage soldier's bulging crotch, and his hand is squeezing and stroking mine. I am terrified that one of his companions will wake up and see us and at the same time I am so driven by lust that nothing could stop me. Inch by inch I unzip his fly; inch by inch I ease his great big thick hard hot amber-smooth uncircumcised dick out of the opening I have made in his uniform's trousers. Goran's gigantic prick sticks out of his khaki fly, his cock's beautiful pink uncircumcised glans already protruding, exuding musk and young male sexual desire, drooling with his smegma and prostatic fluid that gleams in the moonlight filtering now through the dirty train window. I stare in wonder and lust at his beautiful swarthy staff of flesh, its smooth rosy cockhead glistening with penile fluids. His dick is huge. As long and thick and hard as any porno star's. I grasp his great big black-haired meat and feel its size and hardness. Very slowly, gently, I stroke the foreskin up over his leaking glans and then back to reveal his bulbous knob in its fragrant, wet glory. Goran's cockhead is full and round, a perfect shade of penis pink. The tips of my fingers lightly stroke the shaft of his big prick. I squeeze it, stroke it, savoring how it fills my hand. His shaft is thick, long and very hard. His black pubic hair is abundant, curly and coarse. I extract his balls as well. They are smooth, round and tender.

I take the tip of his prick in my mouth and tongue his foreskin, trying to push my oral love muscle under the skin of his cock flesh, caressing his meatus and his warm, wet, male-smelling glans. I get my tongue under his foreskin and feel his tender cock flesh slippery with viscous juices against my tongue. I lap his cheesy sweet musk honey, savoring its soldier-boy flavor. I am sucking the teenage boy's cock! As I first take his hard, hairy dick with its scent of young crotch into my mouth I think to myself: "This is really happening. I am sucking Goran's cock. This really counts as sex with a Serb!" I am amazed, grateful, excited, and hopeful that I will get to swallow his sperm. I am still nervous that one of the other soldiers will wake up and catch me giving this boy-man a blowjob, but soon I am too into it to care.

I get his dusky shaft all the way down my throat. I relax into long, slow, rhythmic mouth strokes. The soldier boy leans back, puts his hands behind his head, and watches me, intent and unsmiling, as I suck his dick. I take a breather to lick his heavy, round ball sac and rub my lips in his crotch-fragrant, black pubic hair. I untuck his military shirt and reach up under his undershirt to caress his moist, hairy armpits. I feel his chest, which has a small patch of sparse hair between his two smooth pecs with their small, sharp, tender nipples, but I never actually see that hair, I just caress it and run my hands and fingers through it as his flat belly twitches. His belly is hard and muscular, although the definition of adulthood it not yet present. The flesh is smooth as a child's. As I bob my head up and down on his big hard manhood I think that he is probably longing for the day when his flesh will be hairy and defined like a man's, and yet it is precisely now with the fresh bloom of teenage youth that he is more attractive than he realizes. I pull back his foreskin and observe his fat, dark pink glans, slick and wet with spit and smegma and pre-cum. I dive down onto the dick flesh and suck some more. I am terribly excited licking his cock shaft, feeling his teenage maleness penetrate my mouth over and over. I rub my face in his pubic hair as his prick plunges down my throat. I relish his genital flavor, the wonderful smell of a young man's crotch. I am so excited by the scene that I take his gigantic cock all the way without gagging, and although I know my throat will be bruised, I don't care. His rampant male sexuality is all I can think of, all I want.

The incredible excitement of what I am doing to this hot young teenage soldier in this reeking railroad car full of snoring males makes my dick harder and harder. I feel my dick straining and pulsing against my underpants. My crotch is beginning to tingle with pressure. Do I have to pee? No! I'm going to cum! Oh my God. I'm going to shoot all over myself in my own pants and there is nothing I can do to stop it. The tingling pee-pressure builds even more and then instantly I feel hot wet warmth flooding my crotch as I bury the soldier's cock deep down my throat.

I redouble my efforts to make Goran cum in my mouth. His dick feels extraordinarily smooth and hot as it fills me with his topaz-gold hardness. I shove his cock all the way down my throat again and again, rubbing my nose into his dark black pubic hairs. I feel his foreskin tickling my uvula as I shove his prick into my sucking mouth. I take his cock in my hands and stroke it, sticking my fingers into his foreskin, pinching the thick cockflesh and rubbing the wet, smegma-coated glans. I go down on him again, this time using my saliva-slick fist to supplement my mouth, stroking his erect pole with my fist as I caress it with my lips, tongue and mouth. My head goes up and down on the teenage soldier's cock. He would thrust his pelvis into my face if he dared to move, but while I am against the wall, if he were to thrust into me the snoring soldier on his left might wake up. I glance up at him for a moment, his dick still in my mouth; his expression now is one of concentrated desire. He is close to cumming in my mouth. Soon he will be spurting his hot wet teenage soldier slime, gob after gob of viscous young semen, floods and torrents of adolescent sperm, filling my mouth, coating my throat, shooting down into my welcoming stomach. I keep sucking and jacking his cock up and down, savoring the feel of his tender young pubic hair and crotch beneath my exploring fingers, the odor of his sweating young eighteen-year-old flesh, his hard boy's dick fucking my face.

His penis swells up even longer, thicker, and harder than it was. I feel his meatus dilate on my tongue. Suddenly he hits my head! At the same moment I feel my mouth filling with a new musky moistness, thin at first but getting thicker and more plentiful. Goran is cumming in my mouth! He cums and cums and cums, spewing his hot, sweet, thick, Serbian soldier juice into my mouth and down my throat. My mouth is bathed in warm, slippery, salty-sweet, soldier-boy sperm. Goran's cum is pumping out in huge blobs and spurts. Long ropey strings of his hot young semen fill my mouth. I am swallowing frantically to keep up with the copious load that his prick just keeps dumping and dumping and dumping into my mouth. He keeps on cumming, heating my mouth and coating my tongue, teeth and throat with his sloppy, slimy, white, thick, male juice. Finally after irrigating my buccal tract with yet more squirts and globs, he pulls his supersensitized dick out of my mouth to give it a rest. It is still hard and now shining with spit and jism and bobs up and down with readiness for more action. He brought his hands down hard, involuntarily, at the moment the ejaculation started. He whispers an apology even as I am still licking the clear white fluid from his shining hard thick dick. My mouth full of Serbian soldier sperm, I swish his semen around in my cheeks to savor it before swallowing while he still breathes heavily with the aftershocks of cumming, his panting covered up by his snoring fellow-soldiers and the clackety-clack of the train wheels as we rush through Southern Serbia.

I slowly begin to lift my face from his crotch, but he grabs me and shoves my head back down on his dick to fuck my mouth again. I am chowing down on his humungous baby-maker taking his stiff, long cock all the way to the hilt, thrusting my nose into his pubic hair, savoring once more the young man smell of his crotch. Just before he cums I grab his dick with both my fists so that even as he shoves violently in orgasm his semen floods into my mouth rather than down my throat. I want to hold his man fluid there, relish it, enjoy it. My Serbian soldier boy is still gushing gallons of goo, hot and thick, trickling uncontrollably down my ecstatically gorged throat. But as soon as his military prick has spouted its last spasm of sperm into my mouth he pulls it away, puts it in his pants, zips up his fly, tucks in his shirt, crosses his arms on his chest, leans his head back and begins to snore almost immediately.

The train pulled into Kumanovo around five that morning. The dawn was cool, moist, grey, and I had the best sore throat I have ever felt. Goran said good-bye to everyone in the compartment, shaking hands with his comrades and also with me. He didn't give any indication that anything had happened between us. I never saw him again, and by now he has undoubtedly lost his looks, his greying hair falling out, his face lined with the cares of raising a family, his body bloated from greasy food and not enough exercise, but in my mind he will always be the handsome young soldier whose cock I sucked that magical night on the Orient Express.

SOLDIER BOY

WILLIAM COZAD

"**W**HERE'S CHINATOWN?"

"I don't know," the young man said.

"Well, you go down Market Street and turn left onto Grant."

He laughed. He was a baby-faced kid wearing an Army field jacket. He had close-cropped brown hair and large brown eyes.

"Why did you ask me? I didn't want to know where it was."

"It was just an excuse to talk to you."

"You're not an MP?"

"What's that?"

"Military Police."

"Nope. Why?"

"I just wondered."

We were standing by the cable car turnaround at Hallidie Plaza in downtown San Francisco. That was strange, what he asked about the Military Police. He didn't look like a soldier, although I figured him around nineteen, chicken delight. His jacket was unzipped and he was wearing a mesh black shirt that showed his smooth chest and small brown nipples. He was wearing white Reeboks.

"Where are you from?"

"Monterey," he said.

"That's beautiful country. Carmel-by-the-Sea is gorgeous. Of course it's a tough place now that Clint Eastwood is mayor, huh?"

"I guess so."

I couldn't figure this kid out. He seemed kind of nervous but he made no excuse to get away from me.

"I was just going to Chinatown to get something to eat. Want to join me?"

"Uh, no. But thanks anyway."

He was a strange one. Maybe he was broke, most kids were.

"I'm buying."

"That's different. Let's go. I'm sorry, man. I'm broke. But I'd like something to eat."

28

"Ever been to Chinatown?"

"No."

"Chinese food tastes better in the Orient, especially the number three."

He gave me a puzzled look.

San Francisco had the largest Chinatown in the U.S. As we strolled along Grant Avenue, the main street, there were shops selling robes, gold and jade, and stores with smelly seafood and odd looking veggies. There was the sound of Chinese music and the singsong talk of Chinese people.

"This is like another world," he said.

"What's your name."

"Grady."

I wasn't sure if that was his first or last name but it didn't matter. I told him my name.

I led him to a restaurant on Jackson Street that was down below street level, where Chinese people ate, not a tourist place. I'd been there often, the food was good and not expensive.

In the booth, Grady looked at the menu. It was in Chinese, there was a section on the back in English.

"What would you like?"

"Beats me. I don't know what all this stuff is."

"Try the combo, you get everything, fried rice, chow mein, egg roll and shrimp. You get tea and fortune cookies."

I thought of the gay Chinese restaurant that they said served cum of some young guy but I didn't tell Grady about that, didn't want to scare him off. Or that they called a gay Chinese chew-man-chew. Some people have no sense of humor.

Grady ate the food with a fork while I managed chopsticks just to show off.

"Tastes good, all the vegetables."

"You're hungry again in about an hour," I said.

I bit my lip to keep from saying that after you eat a Chinese guy, you want another one in about an hour.

"I'm full now," he said. "Do you have a smoke?"

"No, I gave it up."

I got the elderly waitress to get Grady a pack of Marlboros.

"Thanks, man. I owe you."

"Forget it."

Of course I was licking my chops like the wolf in front of the hen house.

"Do you eat in Chinatown often?"

"Yeah. I live on the edge of it."

"You like it there?"

"Yeah. Chinese people mind their own business. They're smart too. Lot of Chinese money is buried in San Francisco because of the British lease expiring on Hong Kong, so the government don't take their money. Chinatown is expanding into North Beach, they're buying up the real estate from the Italians."

"You know a lot about it. What do you do?"

I go down on you, I thought, but kept from saying it.

"I'm a student at State and work in a bookstore."

I spared Grady the sordid details, that it was a porno bookstore downtown that hustled porn to Japanese tourists mostly because they lost face if they bought it in the Ginza, the red light district of Tokyo. They'd hide the simulated sex films in their dirty laundry to get it past Customs.

"I was thinking about going to college later on."

"It's an investment in the future."

I didn't believe that so much anymore, after all the crap I listened to in classes and all the unrelated facts I had to learn.

"I'm in the Army. But I'm AWOL."

"Yeah?"

That explained his paranoia about the Military Police when I met him.

"Are you going back?"

"I don't know."

That seemed like a heavy trip but I didn't want to press him.

"Open your fortune cookie."

He did and smiled.

"What does yours say?" he asked.

"There's a new man in your life."

It didn't really say that but I wanted to put some feelers out. I didn't mind the investment in a cheap meal but I didn't want to be stuck with Grady if he didn't play. I wasn't going through life looking for memories.

"I appreciate the food and smokes."

"You're good company."

"I'm a little mixed up about some things."

"Ain't we all? You want to go back to my place and drink a beer?"

"Sure. I got nothing else to do."

That wasn't exactly the cheerful response I wanted.

Back in my small hotel room in an alley near Chinatown, I got us a can of Miller beer from the little fridge.

The room was kind of stuffy so I didn't think too much about it when Grady took off his field jacket and the mesh shirt. He kicked off his Reeboks. We both sat on the bed and sipped beer.

"I'm curious, why you went AWOL. Are you into drugs?"

He shook his head.

"Just some strange feelings inside I don't understand. You probably think I'm crazy."

"No, you're just a kid."

"Were you in the service?"

"Navy."

I left out the part that the Navy was more in me. I was a slut. The way I carried on I don't know how I didn't get booted out. I wore my uniform ass-tight, stayed drunk most of the time. I had a strong back then.

"Are you, uh, gay?"

"Gay as a goose," I said.

"I think I might be. But I ain't never done anything. That's why I went AWOL."

"You could get out."

"How?"

"Just tell the shrink that you see cocks everywhere and don't know whether to suck them or climb them."

Grady guffawed.

"Guys turn me on. I mean chicks don't."

"You're really a virgin?"

"The only time I ever did anything was a circle jerk when I was in junior high. A bunch of guys throw a buck into a pile. Whoever shoots first takes it all."

"You ever win?"

"I was the champ."

"Hard to believe, nobody ever hit on you. I mean I think you're beautiful."

31

Grady flexed his biceps.

"I'm too skinny," he said.

"Closer to the bone, the sweeter the meat. You'll do."

"Make love to me, man."

By now my head was swimming. It had to be a dream. A virgin Adonis, butch soldier, begging me to make out with him. That hadn't happened in years. I remembered I once propositioned a cute sailor and said how about ten bucks for a blowjob and he said I'm sorry but I'm broke. I sucked him all night long and money was never mentioned again.

I went to work stripping Grady, peeling off his blue jeans. He wore white cotton briefs. I husked my own clothes. It always excited me to take off a boy's briefs and get a look at his equipment for the first time. Grady's cock was soft, thick and cut. I pulled off his white cotton briefs. I never wore shorts myself, always ready for action, and my cock was semihard and bouncing around.

I got between Grady's smooth, strong thighs. I tongued his brown bush and licked his balls while I held his cock which stiffened. I tugged on his turgid fuckmeat while I sucked on his big balls one at a time.

"Oh jeez, Ohhh," he moaned.

You ain't felt nothing yet, I thought. I love cock and balls, don't get me wrong. But I'm crazy about butts. I like to lick that cord of flesh that leads to the bunghole, then just stick my tongue up where the sun don't shine.

Grady's cock was stiff as a board and all juicy, copiously leaking clear pre-cum. I went back to his veiny shaft and licked it. I held his shaft and dug my tongue into his pee hole, tasting his salty pre-cum.

"I wanna cum," he said.

He was hot as a firecracker and I knew he'd blast a load pronto.

I reached under the bed where I kept a jar of Vaseline. I scooped up a gob and greased up my asscrack.

Lying on my side, facing away from Grady, I grabbed his hard cock and guided it right up my poop chute.

"Oh shit, it's so fucking hard."

Not only hard, it was sharp as a knife. He was too horny and I was too anxious. I had to start over again and ease that big dick in right.

Grady instinctively starting pinching my right tit, which took my mind off the pain of entry.

I held onto his beefy thigh that hooked over mine. He pulled back and started fucking me.

"Fuck me. Oh yeah, that's it."

Grady had the hardest cock I could ever remember. It didn't hurt now because he had my ass stretched sufficiently while he reamed me.

I looked back at him. His cheek was against my back and his tongue licked my sweat while he plugged my butthole.

"Harder. Fuck me harder!"

Grady took to fucking ass like a duck to water. He held onto me tightly while he rammed his big dick deep inside me. I felt like my ass was on fire.

"Oh, you fuck good. Do it, soldier boy. Shoot your fucking cum up my ass. Cream me."

Grady obeyed orders. He shoved his cock in to the hilt and it exploded, blasting gobs and gobs of hot soldier cum deep into my ass guts. I reached down and squeezed his balls.

"Stay inside me."

My cock was hard and throbbing with Grady's dick stuffed in my butthole. I wrapped my fingers around my shaft and stroked it.

Grady started pinching my tits again. He tugged on them while I beat off. He even wiggled his spent prick around inside my hiney.

"Don't fall out."

I bucked back against his pubic bush which tickled my ass-cheeks. And I pounded my prick with fury.

"Squirt it. Shoot that fucking jizz," he encouraged.

As though my cock had heard him, it blasted pearly white cum drops all over my torso. Grady's cock softened and slithered out of my asshole with a slurping sound.

I rolled Grady over onto his belly. He knew it was his turn. My cock stayed stiff even after I shot a load. I kept thinking about this virgin soldier's ass and how I was going to fuck it for the first time.

I didn't use Vaseline. I spread that bubblebutt and laved the hairless asscrack with spit. I scooped up some of the cum off my chest and smeared it onto my randy prick.

Holding my cockshaft, I rubbed my cockhead that drooled pre-cum over the young soldier's tender asscheeks. I rubbed my bulbous cockhead into his steamy asscrack that was wet with my spit from rimming. I located his pink puckered hole and sunk my cockhead inside.

"Owww! Holy shit. Uhhh."

"Easy, baby. Let it go in."

Slowly I inched my cock into the virgin fuckhole.

"Oh, you're killing me. It hurts."

"Want me to stop?"

"I'll kill you if you do. No, just take it easy."

I had to fight off creaming right away. Just the idea of balling this prime beef soldier's cherry butt had me hornier than I could ever remember. His ass was hot and tight and itching for fucking, hungry for cock.

Grady's butt relaxed with my fuckmeat lodged inside. He moved his ass around and fucked back at my pumping prick.

"Let me have it. I can take it. Oh man, fuck me."

I sat back on my heels and watched my cock sluice into the soldier's bunghole. I fucked him slow and deep.

"More. Harder!"

I lay down on Grady's back and bit his neck while I held onto his strong biceps and rammed my cock fast and hard up his pooper.

"Oh God, it's so big, so hard. It's gonna shoot. Do it, man. Shoot your fucking cum up my ass. Oh, sonuvabitch. Ahhhh!"

I shoved my cock balls-deep into the soldier's butt and shot the biggest wad I can remember deep into his bowels. He clamped his sphincter around my cock and drained every drop of cum out of my busted nuts until my cock plopped out of his hole.

"You okay, baby?"

"Yeah. It didn't hurt as much as I thought it would."

I don't suppose it did because when he turned over his cock was hard as a rock.

"Blow me, man."

My cock was coated with cum and tainted with a drop of ruby blood. I got the goo on my hand and smeared it onto the soldier's pubic bush.

I held his thick shaft and swabbed my tongue over his velvety smooth, rosy cockhead and could taste the tangy gunk from my own asshole where he'd fucked me.

I deep-throated his dick down to the balls and inhaled the crud that I'd smeared into his cockhairs that now tickled my nose.

I massaged his hard nuts, rolling the orbs around in their wrinkled sac, while I coaxed more cum out of them.

Grady ran his fingers through my hair and held my head and thrust his cock down my throat while I sucked his dick. I could see my cum trickling out of his deflowered butthole and streaking his thigh while I gobbled his pecker.

"Oh motherfucker, I'm gonna cum again. I wanna cum in your mouth, man. Here it is. Take my fucking load."

Grady's hard cock exploded, whitewashing my tonsils and flooding my mouth with creamy, salty cum.

I lay down on top of the young soldier and kissed his thick, luscious lips, which parted, and our tongues intertwined with the taste of his fuckjuice in our mouths.

After we cleaned up with the same towel, Grady lit up a cigarette.

"You're a hot stud," I said.

He smiled, basking in the compliment.

"You can stay here, if you don't have a place."

"Thanks."

We didn't get dressed again that night. He was by far the horniest guy I ever ran across in my life. He sucked my dick, although he bit more than I liked, due to inexperience. But he made up for everything with his passion and wanting to satisfy me. He even rimmed me in the same rhythm that he beat off.

He was asleep when I got up the next morning. He looked so innocent and vulnerable, like a little boy. I left a note with a couple of dollars, telling him to get some breakfast.

It had been a long time since I'd had an all-night marathon fuck session. I felt like I was nineteen again. I felt that Grady would split and I'd never see him again. He was AWOL and had to deal with that.

When I returned home from work that night, the room seemed cold and bare. He was gone.

The days passed and I tried to forget the AWOL soldier. But I couldn't, especially when I was alone in bed at night jacking off.

One night when I came home from work it was raining and I was soaked. I was tired and in a hurry to dry off and get to bed.

Sitting on the stairs was a man in a soldier's uniform. He looked so young, like a Boy Scout. It was Grady.

Inside my room he told me that he went back to the Army after he left me. He got a month's restriction as punishment but decided to complete his enlistment until he was twenty-one. He told me all this while I was tearing his uniform off. He could see me every other weekend when he had leave, if I wanted.

"Yes, Grady. Oh fuck yes."

CADET COMMANDER

WILLIAM COZAD

I WAS IN THE AIR FORCE ROTC program when I was a freshman in college. I liked the macho blue uniform with the garrison hat and I liked playing toy soldier games.

Although the military didn't have the respect of other students on campus back in those post-Vietnam, pre-Iraq years, I was proud of the uniform, and sometimes I'd noticed other students looking at me in a way that wasn't exactly disinterested.

Besides all the drills, you had classes in military history and the code of justice. The cadets thought of themselves as an elite group on campus. There was a definite pecking order established by rank and a lot of lording it over the new guys, like you had to prove yourself worthy.

The top cadet was Ernie Parker. He was twenty-one and a senior. He was everything you'd expect a military man to be. Tall and slender. Erect bearing. Squared away. Handsome in his uniform with the shoulder bars designating that he was a cadet lieutenant colonel. But what really set him apart for me were his wireframe glasses. They made him look smart, but vulnerable, too. And very sexy. Ernie Parker was my idol. I thought he was a real hunk. I thought about him a lot. Dreamed of him naked with a big hard cock.

During an inspection on the drill field I had my first encounter with the top cadet.

"Your uniform is wrinkled, mister. And your shoes are dirty."

"Sir, yes sir."

My being careless was no accident. It was part of my plan to get Ernie to notice me. I'd deliberately not pressed my uniform after being caught in the rain the previous week and I hadn't bothered to polish my shoes. Hard to believe, since I was usually immaculate, even vain about my personal appearance. I always felt like what you saw was what you got.

I couldn't look into the cadet commander's eyes while I was standing at attention but I felt those blue orbs piercing straight through me, like my appearance was a disgrace to the corps.

During the drill I went through the paces. I wasn't a fuck up, it just looked that way. The detachment officers and other cadets had left the hut for the day by the time I reported to the cadet commander. I planned it that way, too.

I knocked on his door and entered when he said to. I saluted and he returned it.

"Sir, reporting as ordered."

"Well, mister, what took you so long?"

"I pressed my uniform and shined my shoes, sir."

"At ease. I, ah, have been looking at your file. You're one of our best new cadets. Academic test scores are high. How do you explain your sloppy appearance?"

"No excuse, sir."

I felt the cadet commander's eyes on my body. This time I looked back at him, noticing his shock of brown hair.

"You look okay now. But you're late. Some discipline is in order. You're an Air Force cadet, a future officer, and a messy appearance won't be tolerated. Comprende?"

"Yes, sir."

Cadet Lt. Col. Parker got up from behind his desk. I brazenly stared at his crotch. He had a big bulge despite the uniform pants.

"Since you have no negative letters in your jacket I'm inclined to overlook this. Woe betide you if you so much as have a button unbuttoned next time. Personal appearance and respect for the uniform is part of your training. But you need discipline so that you won't forget."

"Yes, sir," I repeated.

He looked me up and down.

"You're a goodlooking young man. Clean-cut. Smart. Everything the corps wants. Discipline and order are a part of military life."

I liked what he said about my being goodlooking and I smiled.

"Yes, sir."

"What amuses you, mister?"

"Nothing, sir."

"Tell me, I could use a laugh. Out with it."

"Something I was thinking about, sir. An old movie actor named Adolph Menjou was on a talk show once, criticizing the

38

host about his lousy appearance — until the host pointed out that the properly dressed actor's fly was open."

"Ahem. Cute. But this is serious business, your appearance."

"Affirmative, sir."

"Perhaps a more personal approach is in order. What do the other cadets think about me, the other freshmen, off the record?"

"Honestly, sir?"

"Speak up, mister."

"Well, they think you're pretentious, overbearing and somewhat of a windbag when you speak."

"Is that what you think, mister?"

"Negative, sir."

Of course I made that all up. The other freshmen were scared shitless of the cadet commander and didn't want to be drummed out of the corps.

"What do you think, off the record?"

"You're my idea of what a soldier, an officer should be like, sir. Strong but fair. An inspiration to the other cadets."

"You're full of shit," he smiled. "But I like you for some reason. Even though you're a greenhorn."

"How much do you like me?"

I nervously groped myself. His eyes were saucers. I could cover it up if he took offense by saying that my shorts were too tight or something.

"Depends, mister. You got ants in your pants or something?"

"No, sir."

"Let me see. Unzip."

I unzipped the fly of my uniform pants. The cadet commander looked flushed.

"Take out your dick."

"Yes, sir." I reeled out my soft cock.

"Looks kosher to me."

"You like it, sir?"

"Yes. But not a word about this to anyone. Can you dig it?"

"Oh, yes, sir. No problem."

"I've noticed you before, mister. Seen you eyeballing me. I could have let you slide. There were other cadets not squared away because of recent rainy weather. But I wanted to check you out some more. I saw that look in your eye. Figured you might like some fun and games with your commander."

"Oh, yes, sir. Anything to please you."

"Get down on your knees. Let's see how good you can follow orders."

Now I was scared and shaking in my highly polished military shoes. I thought Ernie was awesome. But I'd never had any kind of sex before except with my hand, not with a woman or a man.

"Stroke that cock to attention."

I tugged on my cock which zoomed into a boner.

"Nice piece, mister. Do the same to my cock."

He unzipped his fly and reeled out a hard slab of cock. It was big and fat. Drooling, like in my fantasies about Ernie. He was a lean, mean sex machine.

I fondled his hot pecker and stroked it.

"Put it in your mouth. Suck on it."

I hesitated. This was my first time. I was scared.

"Something wrong, mister?"

"Uh, shouldn't we use a rubber, sir?"

"To suck my dick?"

"That's what the teacher in health education said, sir. Protection for all kinds of sex, whenever, whatever, however."

"You're right, mister."

"Call me Bill, please."

"Okay, Bill. Ernie, but that's only in private."

I took out my wallet. I kept a couple of rubbers in there for a moment such as this. I figured it would happen someday, but I never would have thought that I'd ever get my mouth on the cadet commander's cock.

Tearing open the foil, I took out the condom and stretched it over his cock. His cockhead was bloated and the rubber didn't stretch all the way down his shaft. He had a big one.

"Suck it, Bill. Suck my cock."

I held the hard, thick stalk and licked the cockhead.

"Oh yeah, What I like, head. What I've always wanted, head from another guy."

From what he said this was his first experience with mansex as well. We were equals now, rank didn't matter.

I didn't like the taste of the latex but I sure liked the idea of slurping Ernie's cock and getting him off. Good thing the detachment hut was secured for the day. There was just the cadet commander and me, enjoying each other for the first time.

I improvised a little, not having to follow orders. Jacking his rubberized shaft, I licked his balls.

"Oh yeah. Suck my nuts."

I got both of those big orbs in my mouth, all wet and slippery, and I hummed on them. Then I spat them out.

"Eat my dick, please. Oh fuck, yeah!"

I gobbled up the cadet commander's cock. I felt like I'd gag but I was determined to give him a good blow-job even though this was the first time for me. I chewed on his cock. It was hard and spongy and hot. I bobbed my head up and down.

He clasped his hands on my head. I looked up. His glasses were steamed. I had him really hot, ready to blast. He fed me his dick, slow at first. Then harder and harder. I almost gagged but I held on to his muscular uniformed thighs.

"Feels so good. Fucking good!"

My own cock demanded attention. I fisted it in synch while I sucked on Ernie's big meat.

"Oh yeah, jack off. That's hot. Beat your meat while you blow me."

I worked his condom-covered cock with my lips and tongue, practically gagging at times, but I kept it up until I had him on the verge.

"Oh shit. Fuck! I'm gonna cum. Gonna cum in your mouth, Bill. Take it. Take my fucking load!"

The rubber ballooned in my mouth, nearly choking me to death. Tears streamed down my cheeks but I couldn't have been happier. I'd gotten the cadet commander off.

With that knowledge and the feel of the scumbag full of hot cum in my mouth I pounded my meat furiously. Letting out a grunt, I spewed wads of creamy cum into a puddle on the floor.

Ernie pulled his cock out of my mouth and snapped off the rubber, dripping his cum from the condom into the puddle and dropping the spent rubber on the floor.

"That was good for starters."

I smiled at his words, thinking he'd want me to suck him again in the future.

"You've got a beautiful big cock, Ernie."

"You want some more?"

"Anytime you're ready, just tell me."

He pulled me up to my feet. My legs were wobbly. He held me tightly and clutched my asscheeks.

"I want to see you naked, Bill."

I liked that idea. I knew I had a hard, hot body. I exercised a lot and was in good shape for my eighteen years.

Slowly and sexily, I hoped, I took off my blouse, shirt and tie. Then my shoes and socks. Off with my uniform pants, down to my white cotton briefs.

"You're perfect," he sighed, staring at me through his glasses. "Like a marble statue. Not a hair on your body."

"I'm yours," I said.

Ernie held my naked body and ran his fingers in my asscrack, then his middle finger punched into my pucker.

"I wanna fuck you, Bill."

"Oh wow, I don't know about that."

"You're a virgin, aren't you?"

"Yeah."

"Listen, I'll be gentle. I've always wanted to fuck another guy. Just never saw the right guy until now. Until you."

I didn't know if that was just a line or not, but I bought it.

"I want you, Ernie. I want you to be the first one."

"Down on all fours."

I got into position. Maybe that's how he'd fucked girls.

"Gotta use a condom."

"Oh, yeah. I'm so horny from looking at your ass that I almost forgot."

I gave him the other rubber from my wallet and watched him fit it on his prick.

He spread my buttcheeks. I looked over my shoulder and watched while he spit in my crack. He slapped his hard rubbered dick against my smooth buns.

"Stick it in me."

He nudged his condom-covered cockhead into my puckered hole.

"Yeow! It hurts."

"Relax. You can take it."

I bit my lips while he fed his big meat up my hole. I was completely stuffed. I thought he'd torn my ass up but I didn't care. I wanted dick. I wanted Ernie's dick. I wanted to be fucked in the ass. I wanted to be fucked by the man I idolized.

My assring was expanded to the max. He started to saw in and out of my hole. The pain subsided and I liked the sensation of hot dick cramming my hole.

"Fuck me, Ernie. Fuck my ass."

He rammed his cock in my ass. I moved around and bucked back. My asshole was on fire. My whole body tingled like I'd been shot with bolts of electricity.

"Oh, yeah. Fuck me with your big dick. I want all of it. Screw my ass." I shimmied back against him, moaning at the pleasure.

Ernie slammed his cock in deep, pulled back, almost out, then stuffed my butthole again and again with his hot meat. My cock was hard as a rock. He reached underneath and jacked me off while he cornholed me.

"Oh, it's so big. So hard. It's gonna shoot. I can feel it. Oh my God, hot cum up my ass. Aw fuck!"

His big balls slapped against mine. He tugged on my prick while he shot his load into the rubber up my bunghole.

Feeling his fiery jism in the rubber up my ass and feeling his hot hand masturbating me took me to the brink. I let go with a shattering climax. My whole body shook while I gushed gobs and gobs of jizz onto the floor and my asshole spasmed around the cock embedded in it.

Ernie withdrew his cock from my ass and peeled the rubber off it and let the load leak onto the floor. "That was something else!" he said.

His glasses were steamed up again but the mist soon evaporated. He tucked his big meat back into his uniform pants. He cleaned up the mess on the floor and flushed it in the nearby john.

I managed to get back into my uniform. I was all hot and sweaty but I couldn't have been happier.

Ernie and I continued to carry on, in secret. I fell in love with him and I sensed that he felt the same way, but he never said the words. If the other cadets sensed there was anything between me and the cadet commander, no one ever said anything. I tried to cool it, but I'm sure the gleam in my eye and the glow in his presence made it obvious to anyone who was discerning.

At the end of the term Ernie graduated with his commission and went on active duty. He's stationed at Clark Air Force Base in the Philippines, and he still keeps in contact.

Me? I decided to quit Air Force ROTC in protest against the military's lousy discrimination against gays. I even joined a gay rights group on campus, and started making speeches. I don't think anyone should ever have to hide what he is, especially a guy as beautiful as my cadet commander.

FIRST CLASS MARINE

RICK JACKSON, USN

I WAS ALL FOR XO's new "alternative uniform policy," but then I saw what it meant. We had been underway en route to the Gulf for about three weeks. By the time we left Hong Kong on 17 July, the AC units were straining just to keep the interior of the ship under 100°. Of course we didn't know Saddam was going to invade Kuwait two weeks later, but we were already scheduled for a six-month deployment anyway. Floating about the Middle East in August and September wearing our regular dungarees would have been hell. The new ship's t-shirts and soft cotton shorts we Navy guys were being allowed to wear were cool and functional, and felt more as though they belonged at summer camp than in the Nav.

The marines were the problem. Our ship is an LST, so about half the 500 dicks aboard swing off marines. *They* weren't authorized our preppy alternative; they had to stick with olive t-shirts and UDTs — khaki-coloured shorts designed more for wearing under water than aboard ship. In fact, that's what UDT stands for: "Underwater Diving Trunks." The trouble with the t-shirts and, especially, the UDTs was the way they fit when they weren't soaking wet. Picture 268 young men in their prime, stuck on a ship for six months with no job but to work out. The bastards roll out around 0600, chow down, lift until lunch, do laps on the flight deck until time for PT at 1400, and then spend their off time back in the weight room on the Universals. Then picture these guys stuffed into t-shirts they'd been given as scrawny boots before their washboard bellies and massive pecs had developed. The shorts were worse because they didn't cover dick — almost literally. The things might hang below the crotch of a normal human being, but marines aren't nearly normal. Their butts are built better than their biceps. Picture Michelangelo's *David* for starters. Take that perfect, pale stone ass and pump it up with another six or eight pounds of coiled, carbon-tempered muscle to lift and define it into the world's juiciest bubble-butt. Then pretend that it's harder than mere marble and you have an *average* ass around the *Barbour County*.

These guys have so much muscle reaching out in back, grinding together as they walk, that the hem of the shorts comes just about down to the spot where butt meets thigh. Since so much material is used to cover their tight marine butts, the crotches ride up, snagging their dick and balls in a cotton hit-and-run vice that keeps them hopping. Just watching one of the gorgeous bastards sit is a jerk-off exercise in comedy. The butt flares out as he bends, drawing up the crotch to crush swollen nuts up into his body. Then, just when he thinks the torture is over, the seams try to twist his dick off at the stump.

Yeah, I *know* all this sounds as though life would be good — a six-month beefcake cruise. You'll remember, though, that the Navy has a thing against faggots. Those of us who want to pay off car loans or just not get bounced into unemployment lines are supposed to keep our twitches under cover. Hiding a stiff dick in baggy dungarees isn't hard; keeping nine inches of swollen lust a secret when you're wearing thin cotton shorts is another story. Remember, too, that these marines are always around — sweating bare-chested on the flightdeck, walking up ladders with their grinding asses ten inches from a guy's face, stroking around berthing compartments naked, rough-housing in the chow line in their pumped-up pool-boy threads. You try to look away from the asses and just see the back of hard thighs leading up to glory. The only legal solution is to take yourself in hand until the gods find time to strike you blind out of mercy.

After a week of the new uniform, I was spending most of my free time jacking one load after another down the head — and not getting anything but a very well developed right arm out of the exercise. The real pisser was that I *knew* X% of the grunts on board craved sailor dick up their butts in the worst way. I won't debate what number X is — but it's no accident marine posts tend to have leather bars nearby. Shit, in my four years in the Nav, I'd already reamed out enough tight fox-holes ashore to *know* what they wanted. Giving it to them underway was so risky as to be suicidal, but finally I knew I had no other choice.

I decided to start with the nearest marine at hand: a kid who worked with me. He had been the central focus of my palm-drive fantasies anyway, so I figured he should also share the benefits of my new sexual glasnost. The guy's name alone was enough to inflate my crank; it sounded like a refugee from a Louis Lamour novel: Cash Courtreal. Cash was a PFC with privates that defined what "first class" should mean. Despite the name, he'd grown up in California and neither chewed nor listened to twangy music. He had bright blue eyes, a strong jaw, classic brow, and better everything else. At about 5'11", he was a tad shorter than me but had massive shoulders, perma-hard tits, and a chest that went on for fucking ever. Even on *Barbour County*, where the wimps are studly, men came to him for advice on lifting. Cash was bright, glib, easy going, and generally built so fine I'd have licked his mama's pussy just because he'd once passed through.

Getting him to put out was such simple grunt psychology I won't bore you with the details. Everyone talked of little but the ship's rampant horniness so working around to the solution was a snap. I came up with the idea of a friendly wrestling match — where the loser agrees to spread wide. I might not have been able to take him in a fair fight, but this wasn't fair. For one thing, Cash *needed* to lose because most marines are born bottoms. Besides, doing anything in his UDTs meant smashing his nuts to jelly. We horsed around for about three minutes and then I got serious. Cash got his balls jammed; I pinned his ass to the deck and was declared the winner. All the marines spent time readjusting their gear trying to get comfortable; but as Cash lay on the floor of the ET shack, panting like a fiend and shifting his load around, I couldn't miss the rise in his rod. I gave him a playful kick in the butt as I stood up and told him to meet me outside the gear locker on the reefer decks at taps. No space on a ship is guaranteed private, but that gear locker was close. After taps, the place is deserted. The hatch was one of those old-fashioned affairs latched down by six dogs so that if some idiot did come down in the middle of the night to fetch a bucket or something, we'd be able to play dog zero long enough for us to stash our dicks.

The horny grunt was early. I showed up at 2155 and found him with his nerves frayed and basket bulging. We were inside with the hatch dogged before I could say "Suck my dick, bitch." He gave me some shit about how that wasn't part of the bet, but we both knew shit was all it was. My nine thick inches were already sticking out of my shorts, ready for rough marine love. All I needed was a firm hand on the back of his jarhead to slide his foxy little mouth down over my swollen joint. Once the ice was broken and we both knew where we stood, Cash didn't bother even pretending he wasn't the original slut of creation.

While he was sucking at the tip of my dick, scarphing down the pre-cum that was already oozing out of my cum-slit, I lost my t-shirt and shorts. As soon as he'd cleaned up on my backlog of love, Cash's spit-slicked lips eased down across my throbbing head. Swollen with weeks of frustration and hours of anticipation, the super-tender skin of my head had never been stretched so tight. Every groove in Cash's lips tore across my meat like a chain saw through a prayer meeting and sent shivers rocketing up my spine.

My hands were both on Cash's head now, grinding and twisting his face onto my pole as though I could screw him down to find satisfaction. His hands messed with my nutsack and slid back to my butt, to steady his face against my crotch against the lurching of the ship. LSTs roll like bastards, but as long as I was rolling my bone into Cash's cute marine face, I wasn't about to object.

Hoping that the engine noises and the insistent whir of the ventilator fans would muffle my love, I heard one low moan after another bubble up from deep within me and reverberate through the small iron space. His mouth was so wet and hot and eager, though, sliding down across my head and on down my shank, that I'd have risked anything for more.

His tongue tickled the underside of my dick, but the way his gullet opened wide to take my head really proved he'd gotten his cocksucker quals signed off. Cash kept bobbing up and down on a thick layer of slick spit mixed with my own pre-cum, but his throat stayed plenty tight enough to keep my swollen trigger-ridge from slipping past. He hung on hard to my ass as he picked up speed, suction, and pressure.

Against my will, my butt started clenching from the purest of reflex actions, instinctively helping to pump my jism out where it belonged. The roll of the ship bred a counterpoint in the roll of my hips as they crammed my thick dick farther and faster down my young marine buddy's tight throat. Now he was grunting as loud and often as he could manage with a faceful of squid dick.

Not content with my dick, he'd cracked open his UDTs and

was pounding away for his own pleasure. I had other things on my mind just then, but one look was enough for me to know I didn't want him abusing himself; that was my job. Reaching down to pry his paw away, I told him his dick was off limits until further notice. I had plans of my own for it — later. For now, his job was to worry about getting me off. Unfortunately, I was more or less a gone gander anyway. The hot stench of man-sex in the air, the steady slurp of his lips working on the base of my joint, the feel of his hands clutched hard around my ass, and the bone-crunching pleasure his throat was tearing out of my tool all suddenly came together — and so did I.

I have to say he took my extra-wide load like the trooper he was. As I felt my ballbag full of jism jolt up through my dick and spray down into his throat, I made up my mind that anybody who sucked dick like Cash deserved a reward. I just hung on tight as my stiff red pubes ground into his lips and his perfect preppy nose smeared against my belly. My hips slammed harder against his face with every glorious, brutal, mind-numbing thrust of my joint down his jism-locker. By the time I was finished reaming out his troopie throat, I had a whole different outlook on life. If the marines wanted to stroke around the ship in UDTs, as long as they were willing to suffer the consequences of getting my dick hard, I didn't mind a bit.

When I was finally finished with Cash's face for the time being, I pulled him up by the ears and slid my tongue into his mouth for the longest, sloppiest, kiss on record. He was taken aback at first that I'd kiss a guy, but how else was I to enjoy the flavor of my own frothy seaman semen? As our mouths tangled, I slid a hand down his spine to grab the ass that had been my nightmare and waking dream for weeks. Even with the front of his UDTs open and his dick throbbing hard and belly-up between us, that perfect butt filled out his shorts so fine he needed my special attention.

I pulled myself away from Cash's mouth and whirred him around, stripping his sweat-soaked olive t-shirt and tossing it into a corner. Except for his dog tags, boots, and UDTs snagged on his left foot, young Cash Courtreal was mother-naked and marine-ready for a serious reaming. One hand on his hard, hairless belly pulling backwards and another on his back pushing forwards forced him against the hatch to assume the position. Looking back over his shoulder, he asked whether we weren't even — he'd drained my vein, after all. I gave his ass a slap with my stiff nine inches and reminded him that the prize was a buttfuck — a whole buttfuck — and nothing but a buttfuck. Sure, he'd blown me. He was a good little marine cocksucker, but he'd enjoyed every inch of my dick down his throat. What did he want? A fucking medal?

No, I wasn't just being a dick. I'd learnt long before that marine bottoms like to know who's boss. They love having their asses reamed, but need to respect the guy who's doing it. What I didn't tell the gorgeous little shit was that I *was* going to give him a special bonus — one I'd been looking forward to since following my first grunt-packed UDTs up a ladder and feeling tongue twitch and mouth water. Everything about those butts haunted my every moment: the graceful sweep of those twin rounded mounds of muscle, the way they hung suspended as by magic, the firmness and size and even the way they ground together inside their khaki like cats in a bag on the way to the river. I yearned to shoot the biggest load of my life up one of those tight marine asses, but just then the night was young. I was going to take my time and enjoy myself.

Cash was leaning against the hatch, waiting for the worst. He had felt my meat down his throat so he *knew* it was going to be an extra-special pain in the ass. He knew he had to have it, but he also knew taking me was going to make boot camp seem like a day at the beach. Without seeing his face, I could sense the clench of his jaw, ready without flinching to withstand torture like any good marine. When my fingers slipped between those tight cheeks and wedged them apart, he knew it was time. He was wrong.

I slipped my fingers along his musky ass-crack and every sensation turned me on more than the last. His skin was so soft, yet covered muscles of such incredible definition and pent-up power that holding his butt in my hands was more moving than any saint's religious experience. His ass, a creature alive, wriggled slightly in response to my touch. A hundred other sensations melded together, begging the moment to last forever: the sight of his balls swinging low between his legs, the view of his sweaty bare torso growing from impossibily narrow hips to massive shoulders, the memory of his perfect, uncut dick just inches away.

I couldn't help myself. My nose eased up to his ass to inhale great lungfuls of his scent so that I could remember it always. Once there, I had to taste the soft flesh of his cheeks and they led me by easy, inevitable stages down to the musky, sweat-slicked floor of his asscrack. I had to struggle against the full power of his muscle to get my face deep enough up his ass to taste his hole; but as soon as I scored a touchdown, his ass arched upward slightly to give me more room. My tongue danced about his tender pucker, as though daring itself to drill deep inside his ass to learn what lived there. It took the dare and worked its way into the very center of his fuckhole and down through the first, outer bounds of his body. The same glorious bubble-butt that filled out his UDTs was too firm for me to get more than a hint of his possibilities, but I'd tasted enough to know I had to have more.

I had my head up his ass, so I didn't hear everything he said, but the word "ass-lick" came through five by five. I reached up to grab his nuts, partly to steady myself, but mainly to get his attention. Then I stood between his outspread legs, slicked my joint, put my egg-sized dickhead against his tight marine fuckhole, and asked if he had any last wishes. The cocky bastard wondered whether I could get my dick stiff enough to use.

The next second answered that one forever. He would have stayed a tight-assed marine except for the KY jelly. I grabbed him tight around the hips, reared my dick backwards, and stabbed him in the back. His shithole strained and stretched and, finally, gave way just in the nick. My sea-pussy Cash let out a bellow that should have been audible in Akron and then shut up. The bitch had to. He was out of air. Every muscle in his body knotted tight at once — including those stretched tighter than a parson's pension around my joint.

My hands slid up across his belly to tweak his tits, figuring that if he had something else to keep him occupied, maybe he'd forget that my thick dick was ripping the living fuck out of his ass. His hard, hairless pecs and harder tits were fun to screw with. I got off from the feel of his sweat-slicked tits pressing against my palms, but doubt the distraction was of pressing present value to

Cash. He was seriously impaled on the horn of a dilemma: he needed what I had up the ass, but was I too much of a good thing? The only thing worse that my dick up his butt stretching his guts apart was the idea of losing it. I've had other marines confess the same story — afterwards.

I knew how his nasty little brain was taking pain and using it for pleasure. I knew how my thick dick was reaming his guts to the breaking point — but how he felt complete only with me up his ass. He'd fight to keep that feeling of butt-busting satisfaction against all odds. More to the point, of course, I knew how fucking fine I felt up his hot, slick shithole. I wasn't about to rob him of his pleasure.

Despite the "ass-lick" crack, I gave the bitch a break and just parked my head inside his hole. The rest would come later, but his bootcamp butt needed to come to terms with the world first. Meanwhile, I pulled him tight against me, reveling in the hard feel of his chest and shoulders, grinding the wiry rust-coloured pelt on my chest into his sweaty back, licking the stream of salty fluid from his neck, rubbing my cheek against the stubble of his marine-cut hair, and, finally, sucking on his ear lobe to help him snap out of feeling sorry for himself. When his jaw unclenched and my patented ear-fuck sent shivers rippling along his spine, I knew it was time for me to get going. I hadn't blown a nut in nearly half an hour!

I held on tight to his shoulders as my pelvis curled upwards, rolling my shank up his shitchute like the inevitable wrath of Doom. As I slid in, I felt his slick, hot guts part in surprise to let me pass and then ripple along the length of my crank like the stunned bystanders at an accident scene, twittering and fluttering about as though they belonged, but unsure what the fuck the story was. I was about halfway in when Cash rolled his head back against my shoulder and, face to the overhead, let out a long, slow, terrible "Jeeeeeeessssssuuuuuussssssss" that was at once awful and triumphant. I'd clicked that switch deep within him that meant absolute contentment. I'd fucked him past the mortal bonds of earth and sent him soaring to the heights of marine heaven. Our union was complete; he and his ass were mine.

Now that the honeymoon was over, I picked up speed and reamed my rod the rest of the way home. By the time my leaky cumslit was battering the hard muscle at the blind end of his fuck-tunnel and my Brillo-like were grating at the shreds of his shithole, his butt had come to life. Possessed by a lust he had only dreamt of before, his butt ground like a dervish against my crotch. Twisting this way and that, using my shank to scratch his innermost itch, his finely tuned marine body became at last the body of a man. The birth was a noisy transition. Savage animal growls of pleasure replaced quiet, stoic acceptance. The whir of the fans was punctuated by the sweaty smack of our bodies flying together — and through each other.

His hands reached around to tear at my ass, trying against reason to stuff my entire body up his butt so he need never be alone again. All memory of pain had been washed away by successive waves of soul-shattering pleasure. His howls and grunts and frantic, lurching movements along my log brought back feelings I had forgotten since my first fuck years before. *This* is what sex could feel like — two powerful men locked together, each using the other for his pleasure, both breeding bonds stronger than the brotherhood of arms or the priggish prison of popular prejudice. *This* was what sex could feel like: pure, rabid, animal sex — limited only by mutual need and the frantic lust of the moment. *This* was what sex could feel like: my teeth locked hard into my bitch's shoulder as I used him up the ass; my hands clamped onto his hard pecs, pulling him ever-closer against me; our heaving bodies crashing insensibly together; the hot feel of his guts sliding along my shank as I slicked snicker-snack through his shithole; the tight burning in my nuts, the feel of my dick bulging outward as each blast of white-hot jism jetted upward at lightspeed, and the searing, mind-shattering, gut-wrenching, jungle-haunting triumphant cry of the male animal as he flushes his load of breeder-balm up into the guts of his own kind.

I collapsed onto Cash's body as I slipped out of control. When I began to get as firm a hold on consciousness as I had on him, I discovered I'd fucked us to our knees on the deck. I was still hard up his ass, sliding my tits across his sweaty back, dry-humping away; my load was back-flushing out against my balls with every stroke, but my world felt so fucking fine, I was in no hurry to change. I did unclamp my teeth from Cash's shoulder and slipped my hands down to his thighs to pull his ass against me forever. Soon, though, even that exertion was too much and I fell backwards, out of his ass and onto the deck, panting like the runner-up in a Marathon, and truly content for the first time in weeks.

We lay together, our hands touching but stupefied by exhaustion for many minutes, until the air I'd fucked up Cash's ass discovered he was no longer the tight-assed marine I had come down to ream out. His loud, crude fuckfart ricocheted around the space like a deaf bat in a 'phone booth and broke the spell. Cash started to sputter in embarrassment. I just gave him a look of cool, detached disgust and spat, ''Slut.''

When we were a little better off, I asked him what he'd give me for a blowjob. I'd make my little buddy as happy as they come, but his balls were still about to explode. I would have given his right nut to get my tongue wrapped around his huge, floppy, meaty foreskin. Fortunately, he was willing to bargain. In return for letting me tongue out his cocksock, slurping out the essence of his manhood, and sucking his hard marine weapon until I choked on his load of marine cream — if I'd do all that for him, he'd let me fuck him again. Frankly, I think I was had. Still, it was scheduled to be a long deployment so we sailors and marines had to help each other out. Once the war started and our deployment stretched into month after month after month of pretending to practice for the invasion we were never allowed to mount, we had to mount action whatever we could.

By the time we got back to San Diego the following June, Cash and his friends and I had been through a Desert Storm, typhoon relief in Bangladesh, and I had learned to appreciate those marine UDTs after all. They still don't cover dick, but they *are* damned easy to get the grunts out of.

SERVICEMEN

RICK JACKSON, USN

I WAS DEPRESSED. Only Davy Soares had made life aboard the *Leahy* tolerable, and he was leaving. He was wired about the long flight home from Singapore and at getting out of the Nav. At the same time, I could see that he was disappointed that I was the only one of his supposed friends who'd bothered to crawl out of my rack to see him off. I guess, though, I was more than a friend. Still, it wasn't his fault the bus to the airport was leaving at 0530. Because he was pulling out before reveille, he wouldn't even have the dubious thrill of being bonged off with ''FC2 David Soares, Honorable Shellback, departing'' piped through the ship. He'd gone down to berthing to say Adio to the rest of the guys he'd shared four years on the *Leahy* with, but the best he got out of any of them was a grunt and a sleepy ''Yeah, sure. Good-bye,'' before they rolled back over to sleep. As we stood together near the prow and talked about his starting college in New Mexico and someday coming back to Hawaii so we could fuck each other senseless again, I was already feeling his loss. I'd miss him as a friend — and a world more besides.

Growing up in Nebraska had made him an odd mix. His speech and background were rural America; his genes were Brazilian as the samba. His chocolate-coloured uncut South American lizard was foxy enough to stop incoming missiles. He had a lean, hairless body, and his hunky dark chocolate butt wrapped itself around my joint like no hole on the planet. Those dusky mounds of manmuscle were good enough to eat, but their real glory lay on the inside. His guts trilled up and down my cock like a mountain brook until I'd explode every drop of seaman semen I had up into the parched yearning of his ass. On our leave in Subic, I'd once fucked his butt fourteen times in a twenty-four hour period — and the slut still wanted more. The only reason he didn't get it was that Big Rick couldn't deliver a fifteenth salvo without getting dick transplant first. Davy is a born man-pleaser. The one thing he couldn't take was my hard-headed friend slamming into his prostate. The first direct hit of my weapon launched him off my tool and, before I knew shit, he was hanging from the over-head, going off about what an asshole fucker I was.

Standing beside him, catching his scent on the early-morning breeze, I knew despite our talk of reunion that I'd probably never feel his lips wrapped around my nine thick inches again. I'd never be able to grab a fistful of his black curly hair as I blasted my load into him or let myself drift off into his onyx eyes as we lay wrapped in each other's arms and sweat and sweet sailor spooge behind the locked door of Supply Support. The first time I'd done Davy, I discovered what lust was really all about. Love came more slowly than his sweet, cream-filled chocolate roll, but it was as inevitable. Now we were parting, possibly forever, and I felt like shit. Davy gave me that knowing smile he has and covertly slid his hand to my thigh for one last caress of my cock. As always, he knew what I was thinking and said he'd found a disco I should drop by the next night — *Leahy*'s last in Singapore before getting underway for four months in the Indian Ocean. I watched him drive off into the dawn and into a life without me and went below to start the day feeling more empty and alone than I ever had before.

I didn't intend to go to the Hideaway that night. I was never much of a disco person and gay joints have always seemed more desperate than gay to me. This was the year before AIDS turned up, but even in those anything-goes days, I tended to be a one-man man. Besides, the Hideaway was clear on the other side of the island. As the day wore on, though, I felt even more sorry for myself. When knock-off finally came, I figured I needed to drink myself shit-faced. I knew I'd probably also let some dweebe with a twitching asshole pick me up, but maybe doing to him what life was doing to me would make me feel better. Looking back now, I see that Davy's last gift to me was possibly his greatest. When I wrote him in Taos and accused him of setting me up, he claimed he had nothing to do with it. The bitch never could lie standing up.

The Hideaway was in the Meridian Hotel in Orchard Road all right, but it took me awhile to find. By the time I cruised in around ten, the place was in full swing. The music was louder than I like, but the beer was cold and plentiful so I settled down to get seriously fucked up. Guys started giving me the eye and a few girded their loins enough to put the moves on me, but I still wasn't drunk enough. I still just plain missed Davy like shit on a stick, but kept my options open and told my prospective beaux to try again later. After three jumbo Foster's, the weasel needed draining and I found the john. I found a lot more.

I couldn't miss the sound of randy buttfucking in the works. After I'd lost the Foster's, I went round to check out the crappers. Sure enough, the end stall was aflower with love in bloom. I couldn't see much of the asshole being reamed because a little Japanese guy was porking away, slamming his dick as far as he could into the Caucasian love-monkey leaning up against the far wall. Three other guys were lined up just outside the stall, waiting with their pricks in their paws for their turns at bat. I wasn't especially interested in joining them, but something about the scene was so captivating that I couldn't make my legs carry me away. The love-in was like an accident on the freeway — you know you shouldn't slow down to check for carnage, but some base, primeval urge in all of us overrules the sensitive civilized man and makes you do it. I let my dick stand out of my jeans to relieve the cramped feeling, but didn't go after the fucker until the Japanese guy had finished. When he pulled out and away, I saw that butt staring at me and knew I was joining the line. In the five seconds before the next customer moved in, I saw a butt almost as perfect as Davy's. It lacked the rich, chocolate colour, but nothing else. Built of muscle layered over muscle, those mounds of meaty manmuscle twitched and flexed and throbbed with every movement the guy made. From what I could see, the rest of his body was all right, too; but with an ass like his, he didn't need anything else. I was suddenly surprised to find myself in lust. His spooge-stained hole pulsed its yearning in between anonymous cocks and I figured I might as well add my ballbag full of creamy sailor spooge to the five or ten or perhaps dozens of other loads frothing away inside his guts.

As I waited my turn, other guys joined the line behind me. The slut's grunts and groans of pleasure echoed off the tiled walls as they merged with the raspy breathing and cries in heathen languages as one cock after another exploded inside that welcoming, licentious pink fuckhole. By the time my turn came, jism was running down his ass, dripping off his balls, and making a puddle on the toilet below. Normally, I would have been aghast at the idea of a nameless gang-bang in a public toilet, but that night, the very wickedness of the idea became its prime attraction — until I slid my mammoth member inside those hungry pink folds of manflesh.

I couldn't believe the fit. Even after servicing all cummers so far, that butt was still tight and firm. It was juicier than shit, of course. Every time I slid inside, more jism gushed out onto my balls and thighs, but somehow being a slut for once felt *good*. I found his big prostate and decided to punish this asshole for the fucking life was giving me. I took my revenge by ramming my hard-headed lizard smack into his butt-nut with every ass-licking stroke. That asshole responded by gripping my crank-shaft as though trying to scrag the jism out of my joint. I struck back, grinding my stiff red pubes into the ruins of that tortured, tormenting asshole. My hands crept under his chest and found a thick thatch there to fill my fists as I fucked faster into his frothing manhole. Incredibly, it writhed and twisted up even harder up my screwing crank, craving whatever abuse I could dish out. I loosened one hand's grip on his man-pelt so I could go after his right tit, swollen and throbbing with his need. Fingers of flesh slid slick and firm along my crank, nursing me out of my funk and proving that however much I missed Davy, I'd always be able to find satisfaction.

My nine inches had more or less emptied the creamy goo in the guy's guts and primed my own load to augment the international jism jamboree puddling the floor when life took a really queer turn. The slut wrapped around my dick had been silent except for moans and other jungle noises as he heaved off the end of my lizard. Suddenly, he screeched out, ''JESUS'' and then yelled out to anyone concerned, ''Sorry, guys. The rest of you are out of luck. I've found what I need.'' Just so there wouldn't be any confusion, he reached his hands around and began tearing at my butt, pulling my body closer against his, driving my dick down as far as nature would allow. The shock of hearing that voice broke my concentration and I lost myself up his ass in a terrible torrent of white that made Johnstown look like a Sunday picnic. Every nerve in my cock seemed to explode at once. I felt my heart stop and all I could do was hold on to that hairy chest and tight fuckhole as time slowed to a standstill and my body convulsed in the delicious torment of man's greatest ecstasy. I finally fired my last little whip-tailed semen apprentice; my prime Grade-A US Navy cream started to overflow that foxy ass to drip into the puddle on the floor. I reached up, grabbed a handful of hair, pulled his body erect against mine and whispered in his ear, "You can get written up for this, sailor."

The butt I'd been fucking was one of the many aboard ship I'd scoped out in my three years aboard. Many nights as I lay in my rack, rolling about atop my stiff, loveless lizard and wishing Davy could join me, I imagined how fine fucking those foxy butts I'd seen on the way to the showers or strutting around berthing would be. Every gay sailor, though, knows that *some* men in the Nav, unlike most in the Marine Corps, really don't crave choice dick up their butts. We hide behind our walls of butch reserve and lose the best part of ourselves in fear of admitting who we are. Sometimes we bury our needs so deeply, we abandon ourselves and end up lifeless shells walking like soulless automatons through a life innocent of any dream.

The butt wrapped around my cock belonged to YNSN Derek Sampson. I didn't know it at the time, of course, but I discovered later why he was so good: Davy had had him under instruction. He was a few years older than me, but still fine foxy flesh at 27. Because the Navy ages folks before their time, many his age were already burnt-out. Sampson's feckless, fun-loving, unprofessional outlook on life kept him young — and in constant deep shit. He'd been busted down from YN2 just a few months before for abusing his weapon during a long midwatch on the quarterdeck. The CO wandered out of his in-port cabin and onto the quarterdeck about 0415, just as Sampson was shooting off into his white hat. About the only charge they didn't throw at him was squandering government spooge. After that, the whole ship knew he was a character, but if I'd known then what images he was conjuring as his hand slid along his crank, I'd have been first in line to help him out.

Now I knew what a queer fucking pervert he was. Since he seemed to have had enough dick for awhile, I hauled his ass outside and bought him another drink. Then we each had about ten more. By the time we started back to the ship, we knew each other even better. I left his ass in NX berthing and crawled into my own rack, drunk as a fucking skunk, but moderately hopeful for the first time in weeks. As I passed out, the last things I remember were the feel of our dried body juices caking my crank and crotch and the knowledge that I'd have the midwatch underway the next night.

I called Sampson the next afternoon and reminded him I was an 18-hour virgin. I told him to drag his sorry ass down to Supply Support at midnight for a four-hour ream job that would leave his limp faggot ass in a sling for months. From the way he nearly cooed on the 'phone, I could almost hear his asshole twitch. Once he was there and the door was locked, I told him to strip. His delicious brown eyes sparkled as he peeled his dungarees and T-shirt off to stand naked except for his boondockers. I'll never know why, but the image of him in his boots yanked my crank so I insisted he leave them on while I took stock. His sallow thin, five-inch cock wasn't much compared with Davy's delicious chocolate dork, but it wasn't his cock I was interested in. His sensuous lips and the thick carpet of chestnut-coloured fur that ran from his firm pecs down across a washboard belly to his crotch were a major turn-on. Just to show I was more than a stiff dick and was willing to put up with foreplay, I knelt at his feet and inspected his gear. He already had a glistening drop of pre-cum lurking in his lizard's single eye, waiting for my tongue. I inhaled everything he had. It wasn't Davy's thick, musky Nebraska cob, but his balls were the plum-sized nuts of a man. If his ass didn't lose its touch, he would work out just fine.

As my tongue slathered along the underside of his prick, I felt his hips nuzzle my pubes and the tip of his dick tickle the back of my mouth. I slid my mouthorgan back to work on his head and cranked my suction up from maximum into overdrive. I spread his cheeks wide for my hand to fondle the hole I was about to ravage. His butthole and cockhead throbbed his racing heart's passion on either side of his body while his hips slipped his cute little lizard along my bumpy tongue and worked by easy degrees towards delight. I thought for a moment about slurping down his load but decided I'd wait. There would be plenty of other loads before any of us saw Hawaii again. I was going to start out right: in the saddle.

Just as I felt his cadence grow erratic and his ballsack rise into firing position, I slid my face off his prick and lapped the musky scent of man from his balls. Then I stood beside him, ran my hand back across his pelt, and pushed his head down where it belonged. His cock mayn't have been much, but he knew what to do with one. His hot, wet mouth bubbled with drool as he slathered his lips across the great purple knob atop my manshaft. His tongue-tip slid into my cum-slit, hungry for the inevitable protein injection. His face slowly slid down across my meat until, unwilling to wait another moment, I fucked deep down his throat and started to use him like the slut he was. Like his butt, that tender throat closed around my cock and squeezed until I knew for sure he was a quality two-holer who was good enough to take my mind off my troubles for the next four months — and maybe, if he worked very hard, even beyond. His bitch lips gnawed my bone as his tongue stripped my loss away and he sucked me happy. His paws kneaded my balls and cupped my butt and, finally, flitted across my quivering flesh as though I were a stallion at the starting gate and he the rookie jockey determined to ride me across the finish line. "Maybe someday, bitch," I thought to myself, "but not today."

I pulled my head out of his throat and pried him off my dork. A hungry flick of his tongue across his lips told me he'd hoped to chug my jism by the gallon, but I wasn't much interested in what he wanted. I was in charge of this fucking evolution and intended to satisfy myself first. My stiff dick was still dripping with YN drool, his hot, hungry hole was waiting for some action, so I spun his ass around and went to work.

He'd been tight the night before, but he'd also just had most of Southeastern Asia up his ass. Now he was a dick blister waiting to happen. His ass proved his eagerness by nipping at my lizard's snout, but flesh can only stretch so far. I knew he could eventually take me up his ass, but I didn't want to hurt the guy. Even YN's may have some feelings. Apparently he didn't have enough to overcome the lust that drew him to my dick, though. He grunted at me not to worry about him. The slut said he wanted me up his butt on the double.

The asshole thought he still outranked me! Just as he lunged his ass backwards, trying to impale himself on my man-member, I rammed my ass forward to drive it home. My lizard lunged through and into the tightest single shitchute I'd ever felt. Our bodies crashed together with such force that we kept on slamming, into his prostate, along the slick secrets of his love-tunnel, and into the hard muscle at its end. As our bodies thundered together, the whore let out a yelp that made me thankful for the noise of the ventilators and the purr of the jets, but then started moaning and grunting like a jungle cat at rut. His ass clamped a vise around my pole and slipped into his set routine. His butt squeezed my cock from its base down to the tip, rippling along in counterpoint to the melody of my love. Each thrust was met with a welcoming parry too weak to divert me, but strong enough to apply pressure on the hyper-sensitive nerve endings of my dickmeat.

As I slid my dick in and out of his twitching sea-pussy, his ass extracted a torture so delicious, so delightful, so habit-forming that I could have fucked him forever down the bumpy road to Blisterville. My hands slithered across his furry body, tweaking tits, cupping balls, and generally having a very good time. I'd only been fucking with him for two minutes or so when my passion spurted up from my nuts, a creamy Mt. Saint Rick of jetting jism bound for glory. I heard myself screaming at the slut, cursing his hungry hole for not taking its time; but my hips kept drilling my cock harder and faster down his shitshaft until I was afraid I was so studly I'd fucked myself to death. One tiny corner of my nasty little brain imagined the tabloid headline SUPPLY SAILOR SLAYS SELF IN SEX SEIZURE, but I knew if I was going, I was going happy.

When I finally ran out of spooge, I kept on slamming my point home, dry-humping the bitch through his cream-drenched spunk locker until I felt my randy reptile recover. I slowed down and began using my lips in earnest on the back of the slut's neck. Derek went bug-fuck when I creamed his ass, twitching and moaning, and carrying on like a mongrel bitch in heat — but then I guess that's what he was. I didn't realize until several moments later that my work with his prostate had gotten him so romantic he'd shot his own nasty load up all over his chest and belly fur. When my hands left his shoulders to get a tit-lock on his passion, I found him drenched in his own sailor-boy spooge and had to give him an extra-swift dick up the butt by way of punishment.

Without missing a stroke, I harvested some of his manseed and made him lick it off my hand like the bitch he was.

When the second deluge came, even I was impressed. I didn't know I had a drop left in me. Somehow I came up with enough to content even his man-hungry ass. When I felt the fuck-frenzy grip my balls, I just held on tight, determined to enjoy every butt-breaking moment. I think my body figured if I was going to fuck my life away on whores, I might as well go out with a bang. I saw the rockets' red glare and other patriotic naval fireworks as my cock coughed up another hard-pumped dickload. My balls felt about to fall off, but I was tempted to go for round three. That greedy squid ass kept milking my meat like nothing kosher, but I had had enough of this doggie-style back-biting crap. I wanted to *see* the faggot son-of-a-bitch as I nailed the shit out of him with my Jacksonian joint.

I flipped him over, lifted his boondockers over my shoulders and started in again. I knew I'd have to stay in the saddle awhile this time around before I could give either of us the pleasure I deserved. I even thought about giving Sampson the Slut his soul's delight and letting him up *my* ass. Eventually I'd do it, of course, but meanwhile getting there was more fun so I slid along in my well-worn grove and took my fucking time. We ground on through the night and, whenever I had watch, for the rest of the deployment. I still missed Davy's dark delicious dick, of course, but Derek is a fine second-best. Making love with Davy was like taking a god; Derek is a master of down-and-dirty, nasty, do-anything fucking. The only thing that would make life perfect would be for the three of us to get together. I'm working on that.

SEX SOLDIER

WILLIAM COZAD

JOHNNY CALLED. He wanted to see me. I could hear the urgency in his deep voice. I could feel the stir of my cock in my pants.

Things were a mess since the breakout of the war in the Persian Gulf. Conventions had canceled at the hotel where I worked, which meant I'd have less days, less pay. There were demonstrations in the streets of San Francisco. It got ugly with protesters setting trash cans on fire and torching a police car.

I remembered Johnny, my jock buddy from high school. He'd joined the Army and was stationed at a nearby base. How I remembered him, every delicious detail. He was six feet tall, about one hundred eighty pounds of solid muscle. A shot of brown hair and bright blue eyes.

I'd gone home and jerked off dozens of times after seeing him in his jockstrap or briefs or just plain naked in the locker room. Big slab of uncut dick, wrinkled foreskin. Huge low-hangers. I pounded my pud three, four, sometimes five times, just fantasizing about touching his muscles, stroking his prick and even more.

That night, Johnny showed up at my apartment. He was wearing Army fatigues, cap and spit-shined black combat boots. He was toting a twelve-pack of Budweiser.

The sight of him in his Army duds made me hot. Despite the loose-fitting starched uniform you could tell that this was one muscular soldier.

"Our unit is being shipped to the Gulf for Operation Desert Storm. This is my last leave. Maybe you'd like to get drunk with me or something."

What I'd like to do was tear off that uniform and give him a tongue bath. But I managed to keep my cool.

I drank a few beers with Johnny and we talked about the war in the Mideast.

"You're so young to go to war."

"That's what I trained for, soldiering."

"Aren't you scared?"

"Sure. But it's a rush to fight. I think it'll be a real high. Only thing that bothers me is that I'm not really sure why we're fighting."

"To defend the American way of life. To liberate Kuwait." That wasn't what I really thought. I figured more like the protesters, that it was trading blood for oil. Politicians were liars. It didn't seem right to sacrifice a lot of young lives. But I didn't say so. I didn't want Johnny to have any doubt that I didn't support him totally. After all, he was laying his life on the line. I might have to do the same if the war dragged on.

Johnny was guzzling the suds faster than me. He was getting a heat on.

"You know what I really want. Why I came to see you, don't you?"

"Tell me."

"All my pa said was to be a man. Guess that macho idea got him through Vietnam even though the war was unpopular."

He was struggling with what he really wanted to say. I hoped it had something to do with me on a personal level.

"Is there anything I could do to help?"

"Yeah. What I really mean to say is that I didn't want to go off to war, maybe even die, without really living. I heard that some nineteen-year-old men died virgin in Vietnam."

"But you're no virgin. You couldn't be."

"I am. By choice partly. I might as well tell you the truth."

"Please do."

"I want to do something with you. And I think you want the same thing."

"What are you talking about?"

"You know. Sex."

He wanted sex with me. Jeez. It took his going off to war to admit it.

"It's my patriotic duty to help the troops," I said.

"Just me. I want you to touch me. Hold me. Kiss me."

In a burst of passion I grabbed hold of the hunky soldier. I felt his muscular frame against mine. I heard his heavy breathing. I felt the bulge in his crotch.

He held me close, squeezed me. His thick, luscious lips crushed against mine. I opened my mouth and felt his tongue probe inside. I sucked on it.

Johnny wasn't the only virgin. So was I, except for my hand-to-hand combat and rubbing against some girls at dances in school while idolizing the jock stud.

I sort of expected him to take the lead. When he hesitated, I did it. I opened his fatigue shirt and took it off. I took off his t-shirt and saw he wore a pair of silver dog tags.

He took off my shirt. I unbuckled his webbed belt and unbuttoned his pants. He did the same to my jeans. I kicked off my sneakers while he undid his combat boots. We shed our pants and were both wearing just cotton briefs.

His body rippled with muscles. There was spidery hair all over it, even thicker than I remembered from high school days. My body was smooth as silk, with hair just in the pits and pubes.

He lay down on the rug and I went at him with my tongue. He encouraged me with his moans and by touching me. I licked his neck and traveled down to his chest. I buried my face in the mat of fur. He held me tightly. I licked his small pink nipples, which got hard, and I sucked on them.

His briefs were tented and I nudged against them, nibbling against the outline of his prong. My own cock was stiff. His reddish cockhead peeked out of the foreskin and poked over the waistband of his briefs. His cockhead was glossy with lube.

There might not have been any real need for condoms, since we were both professed virgins. But I had determined beforehand that when I became sexually active and got lucky and found partners I was going to use rubbers. I had a fresh pack of them just for such an occasion as this, though I hadn't expected it to ever happen with Johnny.

I peeled down his briefs and was saluted by the soldier's cock. It was massive, about as long as my own circumcised member, but even thicker around.

Getting a couple of rubbers out of my pants, I gave him one. He started to put it on but I took over, stretching the rubber over his broad cockhead and threading it down the shaft. I took the other rubber and he fitted it over my boner.

"Think we really need these things? Nobody's gonna get pregnant."

"Yup, it's good practice. This is the '90s." Johnny didn't object any further when I went into action, possessed by a desire to make him feel pleasure and at the same time to satisfy my hunger for the young soldier.

I licked his pubes until they glistened. Spreading his legs, I licked his inner thighs.

"Oh shit, that makes me hot."

"You ain't seen nothing yet. I got big plans for you, soldier boy."

I sucked on his naked balls one at a time, then together. He almost levitated when I did that. His cock throbbed inside the condom.

"Suck me. Please do it."

Holding his meaty, veiny shaft, I licked it up and down. I tongued below the crown covered in the condom. Then I got his bulbous cockhead in a liplock and started sucking him.

"Oh, that's good. Never felt anything so good before in my life. Eat my dick."

I was a novice cocksucker in reality and bit off more than I could chew. I choked some but persevered and managed to deepthroat his stalk.

As much as Johnny enjoyed getting his joint copped for the first time, he didn't forget about me. Not wanting to just be serviced, or just being considerate of me, the lanky soldier turned around into sixty-nine position.

I thought I'd cream the condom right away when he started licking my dick. He put it in his mouth and bobbed his head up and down.

Taking a break and jacking on his cock, I encouraged him. "Blow me, soldier. Blow that dick. Get it real hard and make it squirt."

I went back to work, sucking vigorously on the soldier's meat while he reciprocated. Both of us sucked faster and faster.

I felt the cum churn in my nuts. But I held off. I wanted to feel him blow first. That happened right away. He tensed his muscular thighs and blasted. His cock was hard as a rock and it flooded the condom tip with molten jism.

He clamped down on my cock and I spurted into the condom down this throat. I'd never had a better cum in my life.

Both of us got off each other's cock and admired the sperm-filled rubbers, their reservoir tips full of creamy jizz.

Johnny opened us each another beer out of the twelve-pack. We took a breather, both staying naked, eyeballing each other and grinning, have tasted each other's cock for the first time.

I peeled off the rubber and stuffed it into an empty beer can. Johnny did the same with his scumbag.

"Wanna take a shower and clean up?" I asked.

"Good idea."

I maneuvered Johnny into the bathroom. Under a spray of water, soapy and wet, that was my wildest fantasy about him from high school days. And it was now about to become a reality.

After adjusting the water I got behind the shower curtain in the tub. Johnny joined me with his metal tags gleaming and clanging together.

Taking the bar of soap, I lathered his hairy body. With special attention and care I kneeled in the tub and washed his fleshy cock. I washed his balls. I handed him the soap.

He streaked the suds over my body. I loved his rough touch. He washed my cock and it got hard. Seeing me hard got him the same way.

Standing under the spray of warm water cascading down our bodies, we jacked each other's cock. His meat was so thick and big that I wouldn't get my hand all the way around the girth.

He pulled my prick with a back-handed motion while I tugged his foreskin over his rosy, swollen cockhead.

Both of us were panting. I tried to hold back and wait but I couldn't.

"I'm cumming!"

I splattered wads of pearly white cum all over the place. Some of it landed on the soldier. He squeezed my prick and it erupted, spraying all over his hairy torso.

We smiled and rinsed off.

If I thought I had completed my fantasy of jacking each other off in the shower it seemed the horny soldier had some ideas of his own.

I climbed out of the tub but didn't have time to dry off. Johnny grabbed hold of me and squeezed my buttcheeks. Next thing I knew he poked the middle finger of his right hand up my virgin butthole. It was like I was skewered on his hand. Most of my fantasies of Johnny involved sucking and jacking each other off.

He had other ideas.

"Got more of them rubbers?"

"Yeah."

I left and returned with two fresh foil packets. I figured we might suck each other off in the steamy bathroom.

Johnny stroked his prick, which instantly stiffened. He stretched a rubber over it. My own cock got hard, watching him beat his meat.

"Bend over."

"What?"

He gently shoved me down on the tile floor.

"Yeah, like a bitch in heat. That's how I wanna fuck you."

I wasn't prepared for it, but there was no denying the soldier's randy prick.

Holding onto the side of the bathtub, I looked over my shoulder. His cock looked even bigger than before.

"It's too big. I can't take it."

"Yeah you can. You want it. You know you do." He was right about that. In the back of my mind I figured it would happen someday. I'd get fucked in the ass. But not now. Not the first time.

Looking at the soldier holding his hard dick and thumping it on my buttcheeks, it seemed like a good idea. Seeing the blue fire of lust in his eyes made it a great idea.

"Take it easy. Gotta use some kind of lube."

Johnny looked around in the medicine cabinet. His cock bobbed up and down like a cannon. He quickly decided on using some haircream. He slathered it on his cock and put a dab in my crack.

"Ready now. Ready to cornhole you."

"Yeah, do it, Johnny. Fuck me. Fuck me in the ass." When he bore into me, prying apart my virgin asslips, I thought I'd die. His cock felt like a steel pipe. He slid it deep inside me.

"It's in," he said.

"Oh my god!"

"Gonna fuck you. Hang on."

He slowly slid in and out. My asshole sucked, making slurping sounds.

"Oh yeah. Screw me! That's what I want! Do it, stud soldier!"

He stroked my hole faster. I felt his big balls crash against my own while he rammed me. I heard his metal dog tags jingle.

The pain of entry subsided and I loved the feeling of having my asshole stuffed with the hot soldier's big cock. I moved my ass around and humped back. My asshole ached. It burned.

His cock was bone hard. He panted.

"It's cumming! Cumming up your ass."

I not only felt like I was split in two, I felt every gush of the cock-snot into the rubber in my assguts.

Suddenly I realized that I'd been fucked for the first time by the man I idolized and lusted after for so long. He fucked me into the biggest boner of my life.

"Look what you did to me."

I turned around and waved my rod in his face. I stood and he was still on his knees.

"You going to fuck me with that?"

I hadn't consciously considered that, figuring that he wouldn't go for it. But my cock didn't care what he thought.

I quickly slid on a rubber. I got the tube of haircream and lubed up.

It was incredible, the big handsome soldier kneeling over the bathtub, waiting to be fucked for the first time in his life, wanting to be fucked by me. He was whimpering with anticipation.

I was super horny and not as gentle as he'd been. I rammed my tool right up his hairy shithole.

"Aw, fuck!"

"That's what you're going to get! Fucked . . . fucked in your ass! Get back what you gave, what's coming to you!"

I was raving. I never considered myself the real aggressive type. But I was egged on by the power of seducing the soldier and buggering him.

He took it like he wanted it. No big protests. Just kept his fuzzy butt in position while I banged it relentlessly.

"Fuck me," he moaned.

Like he was begging for more.

"Hot, tight soldier ass. Made for fucking. Feels so fucking good."

"Keep fucking me. Shoot it. Shoot your fucking cum up my ass."

My cock was like a guided muscle in the ass target, headed for destroying it, blowing it up. I buried my cock deep inside him.

"It's cumming! Take it! Take my fucking load!" My balls crashed against his hairy buns and I blasted deep inside the condom up his asshole. His sphincter clenched my cock and siphoned the load out of my balls.

Johnny and I got back in the shower and washed our de-flowered assholes. Both of us sprang boners and we had a jack-off contest, erupting simultaneously and shooting sticky scum all over each other. He washed off but I didn't, preferring to let his fuckjuice cake on my body.

I didn't want him to leave but realized that he needed to spend time with his family before going off to war.

After he left I thought about him all the time. I checked the Gulf updates on the news to see what happened. I even called his folks a couple of times when I got real worried about his safety.

• • •

Johnny came marching home with all the other heroes, and I was glad to see him in the victory parade, alive and in one piece, regardless of how I felt about the real reason for the war.

We haven't gotten together again, at least not yet. But he called me and told me he remembered our night together, that he thought about it many times when he was camped in the desert. He says he wants a chance to see if it was as good as he remembered it.

VALENTINE SAILOR

WILLIAM COZAD

WHEN I WAS TWENTY-ONE in my last year of college I
looked for truth. And I looked for dick. Everywhere. I
prowled Nob Hill to the Embarcadero.

I had my share of tricks and affairs. One thing I learned when
I hooked up with another dude was that when the sex sparks
ended, the guy usually went his own way. I had my share of
broken dreams.

But I'm a romantic. St. Valentine's Day had me looking for a
sweetheart. Nothing on campus that I could find. That night I
took a walk on the waterfront. I liked to look at the ships tied up
at the piers, unloading cargo from across the Pacific.

I stopped in a sleazy bar near the Y. The Y used to be a dream-
land to cruise, with toilets and showers on all seven floors, and
lots of young sailors and soldiers who stayed there. But it
changed over the years, just like the bus depot, with gates and
security guards denying access to cruisers.

Drinking a cold brew, I looked at the liquor bottles by the mirror behind the bar, and at the mirror reflection of the room.
Mostly old retired merchant seamen, I guessed, who drank and
talked about foreign ports and days gone by. But all kinds of guys
were there.

"How's it going, mate?"

I was jarred into reality by the sight of the man wearing a navy
pea coat and knit watch-cap.

"All right," I said.

"Whisky and water," he ordered.

I glanced at him. In his way, he was a handsome brute.
Macho looking like one of those Marlboro men, only this guy was
obviously a sailor. And he was young, about twenty-six or
twenty-seven.

"What are you doing here?" he asked.

"Everybody's gotta be somewhere," I said.

"I mean, you ain't no sailor." He looked at me and smiled.

"How do you know?"

"Your face isn't weatherbeaten, your hands are not callused."

"I go to college. I'm doing research on the way the city is changing. Like the fact that the big ships don't come here anymore."

"There're container cargo ships. They tie up in Oakland and unload on truck beds."

"You're a sailor?"

"That I am," he said, and looked down at his big folded hands. I didn't ask if he was Irish-American or Irish or Welsh. It didn't matter — and even I knew that all kinds of nationalities sailed under all kinds of flags.

"What do you do aboard ship?"

"Work in the engine room. I'm an oiler."

"You lead an adventuresome life."

"It's a living. At first I was like a boy running away to sea. Now it's just a job."

"But you get to see the world."

"International whores and bars," he said, shrugging his shoulders.

"You must like to sail. It agrees with you, you look healthy."

He gave me a crooked smile. I didn't usually pop for drinks in a bar with just any stranger. But Arthur — he said that was his name — had my full attention. I didn't think I had a prayer at getting into his pants but I liked the way he talked, his braggart manner. He looked all man to me. And that type is worth the trouble, because if you get lucky, it's like hitting the jackpot.

Arthur bought me another beer. I bought him another whiskey. I was relieved when two o'clock rolled around. The bar closed and I was busted.

"What do you study in college?" he asked.

"All kinds of stuff. I plan to teach someday, and maybe write stories."

"You must be pretty smart."

"I hold my own," I said.

"So do I." With that Arthur grabbed his crotch and smiled. That brought my mind back to the thought that maybe I could swing on that sucker. I mean, Arthur seemed available, and his defenses were down.

"It's been quite a night," I said.

"Doesn't have to end. I got a bottle stashed back aboard ship. What do you say?" he asked, matter-of-factly.

"I don't think so. I can't handle whiskey. That stuff makes the top of my head fly off." I really didn't want to keep up with an experienced drinker.

"How about keeping me company?" He answered, not really asking — it was more like an invitation.

Walking along the waterfront, with the cold wind slapping my face, sobering me up, I became more aware of the hunky sailor with me and wondered what he really wanted. After all, he could drink with other sailors aboard ship.

Arthur led me right up the gangplank, telling the port security guard that I was another seaman as he flashed his ID card.

I'd never been aboard a ship before in my life. I followed Arthur down the ladders, through the passageways until we got to his room. "Oiler and Fireman Water Tender, 4 to 8 Watch" was stenciled on the door.

"This is something else, being on a ship," I said. I felt the motion of the deck swaying under me and heard the hum of the engines.

"My watch partner won't be back for a couple of hours," Arthur mentioned, maybe to put me at ease.

In the small cabin was a bunkbed, metal drawers and lockers. Arthur got a bottle out of his locker and splashed the amber liquid in glasses, with water from the tap in the nearby head.

"Bottoms up," he said.

He gulped the whiskey but I just took a sip, feeling the liquid burn my throat and warm my insides.

Arthur took off his pea coat and watch-cap. His brown hair was short, straight and shiny. His eyes were mysterious and green like a cat's. His body was stocky, muscular from hard work aboard ship. He peeled down to his tee-shirt and white boxer shorts. His body was hairy, which kind of surprised me since his only facial hair was a small mustache.

"Make yourself comfortable."

I took off my jacket and decided to strip down like him. I don't know why, but I sensed it was okay to skip the preliminaries.

Arthur sprawled out on his lower bunk and motioned for me to come over there. I thought he wanted me to test the mattress and springs or something. He did in a way. Right away he put his arms around me and squeezed me.

This was like a fantasy come true for me. We tugged off our shorts and lay naked together on the bunk. I could feel the warmth and down of his body against my smooth skin. I was with a sailor on his ship and holding him in my arms.

I felt his hard cock poke against my belly. I felt the sticky lube from his pee hole. Arthur was just horny and wanted to be serviced. And I was more than ready to accommodate him.

When I reached down to feel his cock I was astounded not by its length so much as by its girth. It was cut and thick around as your wrist. Drooling, just oozing pre-cum.

Bending over him to worship his manhood, careful not to poke my head against the springs of the bunk bed above, I encircled my lips around that horny sailor's ample cock and sucked it.

"Blow me. Suck my big dick."

His prick lengthened and I held it by the head like you would a snake. I laved the veiny shaft with my tongue, making the sailor flounder around like a fish. Boy, his dick was a real sea-monster, that's for sure.

I sucked the young sailor's mammoth meat. His big balls were ascended in their hairy sac and I mouthed them one at a time and then together.

"Oh fuck, that feels good. Real fucking good," he moaned.

I spread Arthur's hairy, muscular thighs and licked them. I tongued up under his ballsac and licked the cord down to his hairy hole while I jacked on his cock.

"Lick my asshole. Lick it."

I scarfed up that hairy crack, tasting the soap and the sweaty musk of his body. His skin tasted salty.

I was surprised that he'd let me tongue his hole, since most butch guys I'd met didn't go for that action. I couldn't really figure out Arthur, except that I'd never had a butcher number that I could recall.

"Get back on that dick now," he ordered.

I serviced the sailor with gusto, licking up and down his shaft, looking up into his green eyes while I choked on his rod and then swirled my tongue around on the spongy head, lapping up the salty drool.

"Suck it. Suck my big dick. Get if off. Make it shoot."

I deep-throated Arthur's cock, feeling his wiry pubes tickle my nose. My own cock raged against my belly. I grabbed hold of it and stroked it while I gobbled up Arthur's cock, jacking off in the same rhythm that I sucked his hot prong.

His cock got steely hard and seemed even bigger if that was possible. It battered my tonsils when he crushed my head against his crotch with his strong hands and rammed his cock all the way down my throat.

"Aw fuck. It's cumming! Take my load."

I felt like a drowning land-lover when he sprayed my throat with all that hot creamy balljuice.

His shaft kept gyrating and his balls kept shooting big wads of jism down my throat, and I kept swallowing, despite the sticky goo that trickled out of the corners of my mouth and wet my chin against which his balls nestled.

"Oh Arthur, your cum is so hot, so salty, so good," I said when I came up for air. Then I sat back on my heels and really fisted my prick furiously. The sailor reached down and squeezed my balls. In no time at all, I threw back my head and groaned out loud.

For a moment I expected the door to open and the crew to catch us, checking out what all that noise was. My cock blasted big globs of jizz that landed all over the sailor's torso, like foam on sand. I just rubbed it into his skin and it made his chest hair glisten.

In a quick motion that caught me off guard, the randy sailor got on top of me. His cock was still a hot gigantic boner. He rubbed it between my thighs and against my ballsac.

Spreading my legs, he lifted them into the air. I knew that I was going to get fucked and fucked rough. But I didn't care. I wanted it.

The sailor spit on his palm, lubing my hole. He slicked up his cock with saliva.

My asshole twitched in anticipation, feeling like it was swollen at the prospect of taking that big sailor-cock inside.

With Arthur it was like "any port in the storm" and he rammed that giant fucker deep into my guts. I just held on, scissoring my legs around his waist.

"Fuck me. Fuck me with your big dick," I yelped like an infatuated college boy.

The sailor fucked fast and deep, burrowing into my hole. I don't know when I was ever fucked so rough. It wasn't so painful but it made my asshole burn. His hands held me in the position he wanted and his jabbing rod hit something deep inside me, no doubt my prostate gland. I'd never felt such a powerful orgasm build up before. And I hadn't even touched my cock; there was just the friction against his hairy belly. But my asshole shuddered and my cock spewed a hot load between us.

The clutching of my assring around the sailor's cock brought him off. Streams of hot jizz ran deep inside my guts, coating the wall of my insides with sailor jism.

Sweaty and exhaused, Arthur collapsed against me. I listened to the pounding of his heart, his heavy breathing. I smelled his manly aroma of smoke and whiskey and sperm.

When his cock softened at last and fell out of my battered hole, he crushed his lips against mine and I could feel the tickle of his mustache.

His cock might have softened but not mine. Despite shooting off again, my cock stayed hard as a rock.

Arthur bent down and licked my cockhead, tasting me and slurping on my bloated fuckmeat. Spit drooled down my shaft and wet my bush. It must have been St. Valentine's Day luck because the sailor straddled my thighs and impaled his asshole on my cock, sinking it up his fuckhole. And it was the hottest and tightest that I could remember.

With my prick entrenched in his hole, he humped it. I held onto his cock and pumped it until it was stiff again. He just kept fucking his ass by riding on my dick. I couldn't hold out much longer. I was hot as a firecracker, fucking such a hot sailor ass.

I liked the idea that the macho sailor could give as well as take. While I tensed my thighs, thrusting upwards, he worked his ass on my cock until he brought me to the brink.

"Oh, shit," I sputtered. "Take it. Take my fucking load!"

I shot my wad deep inside the young sailor. He grabbed his bouncing cock and jacked off while I was flooding his assguts. Then he rained cum drops all over my smooth body.

Pulling him down on top of me, with jizz squishing between

us, I kissed him and held him. He whispered "ouch" and lifted his hot ass off my dick, which was still throbbing.

Opening my eyes, I became aware of the small cabin where the bulkheads had been covered with layers of white paint.

Arthur looked at the gold watch on his hairy arm.

"Oh my God, I've gotta go on watch soon. The FWT will be back any minute. We sail at 0600."

I tried to grasp what he said.

"Where are you going?" I said, sitting up.

"To Peru, with stops in Central and South America. Takes around thirty days."

"I'd better get out of here."

"Hang loose," he said, but he was already off the bed.

I dressed while Arthur put on his twill tan work pants and white tee-shirt which were splattered with oil drops, like my cum drops splattered on his hairy body.

The sailor escorted me off the ship to the gate.

"Will I ever see you again?" I asked.

"Look for me in a month."

"Thank you, St. Valentine."

"What?" He looked at me with that half-grin.

"It was Valentine's Day. I got shot with an arrow by Cupid."

"Me too. Gotta run."

I watched Arthur run up the gangplank. And I looked at the big ship, which was all lit up, with water running out of the bilges.

I don't know for sure if I'll ever see Arthur again. But those cat green eyes were full of promises.

DESERT MANEUVERS

BRENT JAMES, USMC

T HEY MAY HAVE BEEN WAR HEROES and all, but the Desert
Storm troopers had six months off and then worked for four
days — during the season when Arabia wasn't much warmer than
Akron. I'm sorry I missed those four days, but I very deeply
regret the months after the storm when our company was called
in to stand guard duty — in the hottest weather on the planet.

When our unit got to the Gulf in mid-July we started humping
our shit across one stretch of sand after another — in temperatures
hot enough to make the fucking sand sweat. Maneuvers in the
UAE's 135° were unbearable, but at least the Emirates are dry. In
Bahrain and Kuwait, 120° seemed twice as hot because of the hu-
midity and choking white haze. The Kuwaiti oil wells belched out
smoke into the furnace-like air already choked to capacity with
water and sand dust. Instead of blowing away as it would in any
decent Christian country, the smoke simmered to a white, oily
soup, too heavy to rise far above the sand, too dense to creep
away on little camel's feet. Bad news with nowhere to spread, the
noxious shroud wound its wet, choking way across our eyes and
mouths, holding in the sun's heat and blocking the slightest
breeze until the very air glowed with a persistent, palpable, per-
nicious presence.

Our desert cammies were khaki-colored to hide us in the sand,
but were thick as a midlands' twill. Even at midnight, they hung
heavy with sweat; in the afternoon the sweat dripped from our
blouses until we left dotted trails behind us in the sand like in-
continent snails. Even swallowing our required five gallons a day,
we lost so much water that pissing was a major operation. In the
beginning, getting us acclimated, they'd give us a few hours off
around 1400, but there wasn't much point. From our cots and
canteens to our weapons, everything we knew, everything in our
world, was hot to the touch.

Just sitting motionless at 0300, life was unendurable. Humping
our gear along on endless daytime maneuvers across Satan's
desert playground, the men who had come to the Gulf as

America's studliest warriors wilted away to withered Dantesque caricatures.

Sex was the last thing on my mind. That August afternoon, Miller and I pulled watch at a check-point miles away from the nearest other lifeform. The little guard shack promised some minor pretense of shade, but it lied. The half walls and tin roof were as innocent of comfort or hope as the rest of our lives.

I lay panting quietly in what shade there was, making a sweat-puddle in the sand, trying to keep from passing out. Miller, doubtless dreaming of breezes from a time before the Gulf, had draped himself across a window frame a yard away. I found my-self watching the steady drip-drip-drip of sweat off the back of his blouse. My eyes followed the darkest river of sweat down his cammies and into his boots. One idle, unguided thought led to another until I realized I hadn't so much as jerked off in at least six weeks.

Looking back, I don't think I saw where events were heading, I'd just finally had enough fucking semper fi uniform code crap for awhile. Our reliefs weren't scheduled for hours; the air was so hot not even the vultures were aloft to see what we looked like. I said a naughty word, went into the shack to get another bottle of 125° drinking water, and stripped off my blouse and t-shirt. I'd have lost the pants, too, but I'd long since given up on shorts and I knew I'd feel like an idiot hanging out in the desert in only my boots. As I wrung out the t-shirt and blouse, if I wasn't a whole lot cooler, at least I was lighter and more comfortable.

Troy Miller was my sergeant, but no one had ever accused the guy of being a Nobel laureate. His job demanded he keep me good to go, but he was so dead on his feet himself he could barely pant. I saw a tentative, censorious shadow flit across his face, but when he started unbuttoning his blouse, I knew I wasn't the only marine around who wasn't feeling much like John Wayne.

I didn't seriously think of doing him until I saw his naked torso. None of us had been working out much in the Gulf, but Troy was choice enough goods he could coast awhile. Marines break down into three general types: R2-D2, C-3PO, and Wookie — short and compact, tall and well-built, and gigantic but not overly bright. Troy was R2 all the way: only 5'8" but well-designed, usually full of energy with a quick lip and quicker grin. His blue-green eyes and chestnut crest of hair were prime recruiting-poster material.

As I stood beside him and watched the streams of sweat roll from his neck, down across massive shoulders and disappear into the thick, chestnut band of thatch that lives across his strong pecs, my crank started to climb north for the first time in weeks.

Troy had come to the First of the Ninth several months before, but I'd never bothered to find out if he was family. Back before the Gulf, when I still thought about sex, no marine had ever turned down what I had to offer. Usually, though, we tend to be conscious of rank. I could be fairly sure of another lance corporal and dead sure of doing a PFC, but lances don't usually go around dicking their sergeants. Besides, you never know. Troy seemed a regular guy, but he could have turned out to be one of those up-tight so-called straight assholes you read about in the *Reader's Digest* and Jesse Helms' newsletters.

My eyes slipped down to the crotch of Troy's sweat-soaked cammies and learned that regular was the last thing he was. The horny bastard must have liked the sight and smell of my firm, sweat-slicked marine flesh, because his pole was poking his pants as proud and tall as a Commandant's parade inspection. Suddenly, all the molten loads I'd forgotten about for so long bubbled up from my balls and I knew I was going to erupt. I could do the inside of Troy's beautiful butt or the uniform of my country, but the nasty was about to get done one way or the other. As I moved around behind him and admired his powerful pecs give way to perfect lats and then the back and hard, sloping shoulders of a Greek god, I hadn't much doubt what meat was fit for my creamy sauce.

I took my time. Miller just looked at me with his bright, azure, tomcat eyes as I eased my face down to his biceps. A glorious stench of manmusk hung about his body, inviting as an oasis. I didn't say a word. Maybe I was being a Valentino shaikh, silent and sultry; maybe no words were necessary. Our eyes had already asked the question; our dicks knew the answer.

My nose slid along the soft, slick surface of his bicep until I reached his shoulder and my tongue went UA. His hard marine body shivered as my bumpy tongue slid across the perfect country of his shoulders. Muscles rippled and quavered beneath soft skin as I licked him clean, starting low and moving by easy stages up his thick, wrestler's neck. By the time I was tongue-fucking his ear into surrender, his hands were all over me — pulling my body hard against his, sliding along my knobby spine down into my cammies, following along my flanks, fiercely grinding the back of my head forward until my face honed itself against his, lifting my hot incredibly sweaty ass as he locked our bodies together.

Gooseflesh ricocheted across the soft skin stretched tight across his man-muscled frame. Lust carelessly smeared one sensation into the next until our clutching, heaving bone-dance threatened an immediate good time. My weapon was cocked and ready to fire when some passing god whispered "At ease." We had the whole afternoon.

I broke Troy's love-hungry grip on my grunt ass, pushed his panting beastial body away from mine and showed disrespect to a superior officer: "Faggot bitch." His arm snaked out and savagely pulled my face hard against the powerful pecs which rose to meat me, pressing his hard, thick man-tits between my lips.

His naked, sweaty chest ground about in such pleasure even I thought it looked obscene until his tit-stalk found the sharp, delicious danger of my tooth edge. Twisting this way and that as his hands clawed at my back, he scraped that tit harder into my mouth. I bore down and gave him the chewing out every bad young marine deserves.

I was so busy with business that I hadn't been listening to him talking shit and groaning away like a TJ whore. When I crunched down on the tit and started to gnaw, though, the very desert itself heard him scream out in perfect, pent-up pleasure.

I tore into his other tit when the first had been rubbed just the right way — and then left it in ruins to lick my way up into his armpit, the unquestioned font of eau de grunt. His massive arm locked around my head again, trapping me in the wellspring of his sweat and scent and savage sexuality. I sucked dry the chestnut hairs that tickled my fancy and kneaded his ass through his sweat-soaked cammies while I did it. After what may have been minutes but seemed at once a lifetime and but a second, I knew if he was going to respect me in the morning, I'd have to do a little training of my own.

When I got a grip on his nuts, he released his hold on my head.

A quick tug at his tits pulled his face down hard against my wiry, rust-coloured chest fur. Sodden with my sweat, it was ready to scrape against his face until he sucked and tongued and lapped my fur dry and titillated me besides. Standing there at parade rest with the Saudi sands stretching away into infinity and Miller sucking at my body like a leech with a free lunch, I did what any desert defender would do: I unbuckled my belt and dropped trou.

Troy may be a sergeant, but he wasn't completely retarded. His face slid down my pelt to tongue my belly-button for a moment and then worked his lips around the tip of my lizard to slurp up the stream of pre-cum oozing out of my foreskin. For a long moment, I let him dig deep into my cocksock and ease it back so he could get at the love-honey and sweat and built-up musk I'd been saving there for that special someone.

I suddenly jerked it away from him with the warning I was going to dick a different hole; his job was to lick the sweat from my balls and, if he was lucky, lick my nasty asshole until it sparkled.

I'll never know how I held off as long as I did. That tongue on my tool had been lethal to my virtue. By the time I shook him off, I was far enough gone that when I felt his tongue lap at my nutsack and his lips suck my balls down into his mouth, my guts exploded. I was too busy having fun to take critical notes, but I know that, righteous though it was, that nut was unlike anything I'd ever known. My dick was free to frolic, but as my guts clenched tight I was able to stay sufficiently conscious to see one glob after another of gleaming James jism spurt up into the air like some alien UFO space test. A few landed on my chest, but most arced high and wide over Troy's bare back to splatter against the desert.

Once I'd started shooting, I held his head tight, nearly castrating myself as he gulped for air and got gonads instead. The last several globs of my jarhead jism splashed onto his back and joined the rivers of sweat flowing down across his gleaming, muscle-cobbled back. Once I'd started breathing again myself, I reached down for a handful of my sweet, slimy spooge and smeared it where it would do the most good: along the crack up my ass.

My waking wet-dream had been wild, but I was anything but

drained. My sergeant was still between my legs, licking my thighs and balls and crotch; but when I barked at him to lick my ass, he hove on the double. Miller's perfect nose parted my cheeks and gave his tongue room to work. At first, he concentrated on scooping up the fresh marine manmilk I'd left for his lunch, but when that was gone, he dug deeper. The slut's sandpaper tongue slipped between my hard cheeks like a Panzer column. I clenched tight despite myself, but that slutty tongue coasted along the sweaty depths of my most secret country. Miller traveled that secluded landscape like a native going home for Thanksgiving, relishing each precious feature and nuance both for its own sake and for the banquet which lay at the end of his journey.

I was bent over by now, bracing my arms against what passed for our guard shack, my ass arched outward, presenting my proud, pulsing pucker for whatever punishment lay in store. Troy's face just kept pressing harder and deeper up my ass until, like a thunderbolt, his tongue tore into my shithole and shut my dirty little mind down hard. I've always had a thing about tongue up my ass. I read once that if you massage an alligator's belly, he won't attack. I guarantee the same holds true for a marine's asshole.

I felt every bump on his tongue as he drilled its tip into my pucker and lapped at my hole like a spaniel with a new dick for Christmas. One distant corner of my mind heard myself talking shit and groaning in delight. My ass ground backwards into my sergeant's cute all-American marine face, but I was powerless to do anything but enjoy. My body had mutinied and was acting on its own. After weeks and then months of hell, my ass had found a small stretch of marine heaven — and it intended to enjoy it.

He kept that tongue tearing up my ass forever. At one point I came out of a daze to feel Troy's ass-licking lips locked tight around my shithole, sucking hard as he drilled deep. My hands were on his head, trying to stuff that face up my ass where it belonged. His hands fluttered up along my sweat-soaked flanks as he worked, licking and sucking and drilling and caressing me, at once his sleek desert stallion and the luscious man-flavored ice-cream bar he yearned to chow down.

As the milk-colored air simmered around us, drawing streams of sweat from every pore, the heat was so enervating I wasn't sure whether I was passing out from heat prostration or tongue penetration. That tongue was so demanding, so terrible and insistent, my balls clenched tight again; I was only moments away from another desert accident, but this time it was going to be on purpose. I'd had enough of trying to see him work on my ass. The ass-licking faggot had had his chance to do me hard up the butt. If he wasn't going to use his marine manhood on me as was his right as senior man, I'd drill his ass hard enough to strike Arabian crude.

He looked stunned when I pushed him back onto his butt and fell atop him. For a moment, my lips met his and I tasted my ass for the first time in my life while our chest pelts ground our pecs together and our hips poked pricks into the other's furry belly. The airborne oil and the gushing sweat made our hard bodies slip together on the sand until our arms and legs and slick marine bodies were writhing like bait in a can of Crisco. I felt his tits digging across my stiff fur and mine boring into his soft, chestnut down; his hand slid down to my ass, forcing my dick harder against his belly. Then we both knew it was time.

We both had our trou around our ankles, but stopping to unlace our boots was impossible. I lifted his legs towards the sky and slipped my shoulders between his calves. His belt buckle pressed against the back of my neck, but just then I'd have challenged a guillotine to bury my shank up his ass. Rolling about on the ground, he'd pick up a dusting of sand so I slapped his ass clean before I settled my dick against his hole. His eyes flashed with every slap until one bred another and I was half tempted to take time and teach him some manners before I fucked him. Just then, though, I was out of time. We both were.

His hard cheeks clenched tight to pull back my foreskin as I dug deep. After waiting patiently for so long, the tender tissues that lurked deep inside his pucker lurched outward at the first scent of dick, clutching at my cum-slit and urging me to drop in for a visit. A hundred images combined in one as I hung there, savoring a last grand moment of anticipation before I did him: the feel of the hot desert sand on my knees, the clank of his buckle and sodden clammy feel of his cammies on my shoulders, the tight luscious depths of his steamy asscrack, the feel of his strong hands on my back as he pulled me downward to our destiny, the way his lips hung slightly parted, glistening sweat and gasping in rhapsodic expectation. Most of all, though, I remember his eyes: the hungry eyes of a wild cat out for a mid-day stroll who finds a sweet, juicy young gazelle struggling with a broken leg. Unable to believe his good fortune, the cat sits for a time, relishing the delights to come, postponing his inevitable pleasure until sublime satisfaction ceases being a surprise and becomes a present fact of nature.

The eyes were Troy's, but I pounced to end his rapacious reverie with a quick, brutal marine thrust. I answered his butt's craving with a single savage stroke that tore through his tight, tender tunnel and kept reaming on until I was buried dick-deep in his ass, my stiff pubes were grinding the living fuck out of the ruins of his shithole, and my cum-slit was scratching a need he'd kept so hidden from the world that he'd even forgotten it himself.

At the instant we became one, I saw his hungry eyes slam shut, but they opened almost at once. My hips had no sooner slammed his body hard against the desert sands than those blue-green eyes found mine. Now no longer hungry, they were triumphant. His lips moved slightly in a pant or nervous twitch as his system got used to having nine thick inches shoved up his guts. In a moment, though, I discovered it wasn't a twitch. He mouthed the word again: PLEASE. The slut wanted more.

Between the trou trapped behind my back and his boots digging the living fuck out of my ass, Troy didn't have much chance of making a quick getaway so I settled in to tend to business. The first stroke up was almost as fine as the stroke down, but his ass was soon awash with liquid love, slicking my pre-cummed way through his guts. As my hips remembered what to do, I made them our master. They drove my thick, butt-breaking dick deeper and harder down into Troy's trapped marine asshole with every stroke, tearing grunts from him and making me whimper as though I were the faggot-assed bitch getting the reaming of a lifetime.

As I looked down, recording forever in memory every flinch of his boy-next-door face and splash of my sweat onto his chest, I realized distractedly where we were. I'd probably done a company's worth of marine butts before, but for the first time in my life, I was fucking another marine up the ass and we could make all the noise we wanted. When you're used to dark corners on base or a quick poke in the back of a 'track, you don't even think of letting yourself go.

As I shot my load up Troy's ass, I tore loose with all the howls and screams and SHITs I'd repressed over the years. The bitch would have jumped atop the guard shack if I hadn't had his ass nailed down tight. For the next minute or so, I was busy blowing my load up his ass, grinding my bush against his hole, and yelling at the gods to get a gander at what GOOD feels like.

The slick feel of my own jism up Troy's tight marine ass was such a turn-on, there was no way I was about to leave home. I'd never been harder. Sweat was pouring off me in buckets, but at least it was good, honest sweat that I'd done something to earn. Besides, I wasn't getting stuck with it; Troy was the poor bastard awash. When he saw I was going for another inning, he stopped being shocked and returned my boot camp noise decibel for deafening decibel. I'd give his ass an especially vicious prostate pounding and yell as loud as I could into the face three inches away from me: "Take that you faggot, shit-bag excuse for a marine!"

He'd clench the whole length of his shitchute around my massive marine meat and slam back with "Give me something to work with, Needledick." We kept it up, fucking harder and screaming louder like butch marine drill instructors gone wrong as I pounded his body against the bedrock, pushing him slowly across the desert as my dork drilled his ass and his boots rode my butt as though we were at Santa Anita. I'd fucked him dry by the time my next load was ready to launch, but it was the best of the day — maybe the best of my life. The slick feel of another marine body trapped below me in the desert wilderness was almost as much a rush as the tight dry fuck-friction heat toasting my tool on the inside as we steamed on the outside and the glorious raucous marine noise we made as we rutted were the best fucking time I can imagine having. Just before I lost it again, I pulled myself — and Miller to my knees so I could hold him in my arms while I shot my load up his ass. My teeth tore into his dusty, sweat-soaked shoulder and my hands tore at his hard back as my hips drove my dick home where it belonged: into the deepest, most secret reaches of my sergeant's guts.

It was there I left my load as we thrashed and howled in the middle of the Saudi sands like psychotic savages on speed. It was there that I found my true home, my true marine core. When I was finished with his ass, I collapsed back atop him and lay for a moment trying to catch my breath. He was patient for all of a dozen seconds before he said, "All right, lance corporal. Let's get these weapons cleaned." Needless to say, he intended me to start on his. The bitch expected me to suck his dick!

Fortunately for us both, I wanted nothing more. He was trimmed meat, but the horn-dog bitch had been oozing pre-cum for hours. By the time I sucked his balls flat and chugged down his first load of the day, I couldn't resist sticking around for another serving. I insisted that this time around, while I was proving what cocksuckers lance corporals could be when they had a sergeant like him, he should get that talented marine tongue of his back into action up my butt. The feel of that bumpy tunnel tickler is better than any possible narcotic — and impossibly more addictive. My mind slipped into neutral as we used good old marine teamwork to make sure these desert maneuvers came off just right.

By the time dark and our reliefs were due, we were rubbed so raw by the sand and each other, it was time to stow our gear and stand down. Now that I'd discovered what an ass-lick my sergeant was, I was looking forward to the next several months. We couldn't always howl at the heavens while we drilled for desert cream, but we'd be together. Life had turned a corner and was looking pretty fucking good. When the night team showed up, they must have wondered what we were so happy about. After all we'd been through in the previous months, being happy didn't seem natural. After that day, though, together and alone, happiness was the most natural thing of all.

BOOTCAMP BUTT

RICK JACKSON, USN

E VEN WHEN WE DEPLOY together on amphibious ships, sailors and marines usually don't hang out together. Our schedules are different, we sleep in different berthings, and we just plain don't have much in common — as a rule.

We squids are plenty busy underway; the grunts mainly try to keep out of the way. Sailors are often working twelve on–twelve off for months; jarheads have dick to do but work out and wait for battle. Ashore, the troopies have it rough, but an average grunt day involves rolling out of the rack at 0600, chow at 0700, PT at 0730, lunch at 1100, and maybe a few laps around the flight-deck or some time with the Universals in the weightroom during the afternoon before chow and bed. Marines come aboard look-ing choice, but their underway workout schedules would turn a mob accountant into a stud.

As Desert Shield blew up toward Desert Storm, we floated around the Gulf so long that the lines between Navy blue and cammie green started to blur. I'd seen Lance around the ship, but I got to know him in one of the classes the Navy brought aboard. The idea was to earn college credits and keep from being bored as our world drifted towards war. Some squids signed up, but the marines eager for something to do that didn't involve heavy lift-ing, registered in packs. Contrary to what you've probably heard, marines are sharp guys. At first, though, Lance and I had little in common except the coincidence of having the same last name. I'd run into other members of the Jackson clan before, but none of them had been built like Lance. Before we realized it had hap-pened, we were fighting for the top of the class and the prof was making cracks about "the over-achieving Jackson brothers."

I wished. Underway, I tried my fist-fuck fantasies, but Lance made it rough — especially since we were all stroking around the ship in just t-shirts and shorts because of the heat. Every time Lance and his troopie buddies were around, my shorts just natur-ally climbed towards the overhead. Lance was a 19-year-old PFC during the War — and about 6'1" of the foxiest preppy young marine meat you could hope to wrap a lip around. His face was something of a blend between Chris Reeve and Schwarzenneger, with close-cropped temples and a crest of dark blond hair on top. Doe-brown eyes with lashes into next week, a perfect Ivy-league nose, high cheekbones, a strong jaw, and enough sparkling white teeth to make a Hollywood agent cream his trou were just the beginning of his Jackson charms. Daily PT had broadened his shoulders and chest, narrowed his hips, and pumped up his perfect, tight marine ass to the point I'd have gladly licked his mama's pussy just because he'd once passed through naked.

After that first history course, we found ourselves in a couple of math classes and finally one in marketing. The folks at home called us war heroes — but during Desert Storm, Lance and I had dick to do. Even our role in Desert Shield was pretty minor: practice maneuvers in Operation Imminent Thunder, a couple of SCUD false alarms, and a great Christmas liberty in Bahrain just before the war started.

We were half-way through the marketing class when we pulled into Bahrain for Christmas liberty. Lance had been friendly for weeks, always eager to kick back and chat when we ran into each other around the ship. I had tried to keep my distance so I wouldn't warp out and shove my good news up his ass without an invitation; but when he asked the day we pulled in if I'd show him around town, I couldn't say no. At least ashore, I didn't have to put up with the sight of his hard marine butt grinding away inside his skimpy UDTs — the tan shorts marines wear, more designed to show off their butts and baskets than cover anything.

We might as well have been brothers, we got along so well — as long as I could banish the image of his face being skewered on the end of my joint or him bent double, ass to the sky while I used his hole like a cur bitch in heat. This was my second float so I showed the bootcamp around the Bab souk, we ate Pizza Hut at the Yateem Centre, and then spent hours at the gold souk. By the time evening prayers screeched across the sunset, we had shopped. Lance was bitching about sore feet, and sounded more like a pooped preppie than desert defender. Like any good squid on liberty, I suggested we stop by the Holiday Inn for a couple beers before we caught the bus back to Mina Sulman Pier.

Lance was studly, clever, and charming; but the guy had no

more idea how to limit himself to a couple beers than the village dog knows how to conduct Bartok. Even at $4 a brew, we were both shit-faced inside an hour, but Lance wasn't about to let up. When I told him the last bus back to the pier was about to leave, he just snarled, "Fuck the pier." His VISA card appeared as he staggered out to the desk for a room. It cost him almost $200, but he was able to drink for another hour before he got sloppy. I managed to propel him upstairs, out of his clothes, and into the shower before he got really messy. Once I was sure he was on the mend, I left him under the water for nearly twenty minutes, not so much because I didn't like watching him heave, but because the sight of water splashing off the classic male body was more than I knew I could bear. The gorgeous bastard was retching like a bootcamp on moonshine; but anyone seeing his hard, hairless pecs heaving under the cold spray or his massive marine bubble-butt begging unconsciously for what I had as he unselfconsciously leaned against the tile would have seen too much to keep from jumping his humps.

When he'd sobered up enough to dry himself off, I rinsed down the shower, and used it myself. By the time I came out, he was safely in his rack and I assumed, passed out. I was about ready to crawl between the cool white sheets of the bed across from his for my first night ashore in months when I heard soft, wet, ugly choking sounds coming from his bed. The shower should have sobered him up, but the first thing you learn in the Navy is not to take chances with buddies aspirating puke. That Christmas the War was still two weeks away. Nobody was sure we would make it home alive, but the idea of a perfect young animal like Lance being shipped home in a bag because he'd choked to death on puke scared me so shitless I forgot about keeping my distance. I'd grabbed his shoulders and was trying to roll him over before I realize the difference between chokes and sobs. For about thirty seconds, I was shocked rigid. I'd never thought of Lance as the maudlin drunk type. Then, my eyes double-crossed me, drifting from the tears streaming across his cheeks to really notice the rest of his body; I went seriously rigid.

I babbled something about being sorry and pointed my peter back towards the other bed, relieved he was too torn up by whatever to notice my nine plus inches of swollen solecism pounding away, belly-up and ready to wrangle. Before I could move, his hand latched around my wrist and pulled my ass down onto the bed. All sobs and snuffles, tears cascading down his classic cheeks, he somehow managed to sputter, "No. Please. Just — Sorry. Can you just . . . hold me a minute."

I wanted to hold him all right. He obviously had some macho marine male-bonding crap in mind. Since I've never understood EST or encounter groups or even pretended to understand foxhole psychology, I had no clue what he was after or how to react. I let him pull me down to the mattress, but lay stiff and uncomfortable beside him, feeling a little like a prom king at a coroner's carve-up. Not knowing what to say, I kept quiet and just hoped he wouldn't see my joint beating cadence against my belly. He sobbed on, choking out drivel about not being a good marine because he was weak. Clamped onto my arm, he certainly felt strong enough. When I tried to back away, he twisted about, tossing a leg over to trap mine — and giving me the shock of my squidly young life. His dick was not only a match for my nine thick inches of Naval pride, the bastard was cocked and ready to fire. At first I thought he had his hand down there, but his hands were both busy holding me hard beside him. Besides, even through his sheet, the heat and swollen, throbbing need of his first class privates grinding into my flank was inescapable.

Despite sharing the same last name, I still didn't think he was family. Everything about Lance shouted out cocky young marine stud on the way up. He couldn't be gay. The gods weren't that kind; they were just fucking me hard. Then, after I tried to comfort him for what felt like forever, he managed to whimper out the good news: Would I do him a favor and keep it between us. He couldn't let his buddies on the ship EVER know, but — Would I — do him?

He'd have warped out completely if I hadn't; but once I knew how much a Jackson he really was, he didn't need to beg twice. Faced with such need, I knew what I had to do to help out a shipmate. I reached down to grab his swollen service member and used it to shift him from neutral into first. The rough linen sheet was already wet with pre-cum oozing out in a relentless stream of encouragement. He didn't believe at first I was really going to give him what he needed; but when I slammed his body back onto the bed and jerked the sheet off him, his marine instincts recognized I was in charge. The problem was, I wanted him all at once and couldn't decide where to start.

My hands took a slow, careful measure of his flesh. They glided deliberately across his pecs and flanks, and down across his hard, flat belly until he was trembling like a colt and groaning, slack-jawed, like a Tijuana whore. His tits were swollen tall and eager, teasing my lips into tormenting them. Fierce and spit-slicked, they took up the challenge, sliding roughly up and down his nubbins until I was whistling up a desert storm of my own. His broad chest bucked upwards, hard against my face as though eager for the dangerous feel of my teeth and the delicious torment they could deliver. My right hand slid down to his messy, love-lubed crank and held him fast.

With anyone else, I'd have long since chowed down his dick until I choked on his load. Lance was a surprise, but I'd been around marines enough to know what they need: a hard fuck up the butt. I knew before I left his bed, I'd swallow his joint so far down my gullet he'd get acid burns; but first, I had to do him hard. He yearned to be taken, to be shown someone else was in charge. I'm normally a gentle, easy-going cocksucker. I've never much liked being done up the ass myself, and enough men have run screaming into the night at the sight of my Jacksonian joint that I'm usually content with much less than the brutal buttfuck I knew Lance craved. He'd begged for my help; I was going to give it to him — and keep on giving it to him until he had my frothy naval jism spurting out his cute little ears.

I hadn't left the ship with cruising in mind, so I hadn't brought any lube along. We didn't need it. Lance had enough clear, organic lube for the Seventh Fleet. I slid my fist up his crank and down mine, leaving a crystal-pure coating of the slickest dick-do I'd ever worn. Lance lifted his feet off the mattress to show he was ready — but not nearly far enough for what I had in mind. I grabbed his ankles and spread him like a stubborn wishbone until he popped his ass into range. I would have loved to slide my tongue up his crack first, stripping clean the scent of man his sloppy shower had doubtless left behind; but I had to play the butch marine-rapist — at least until he'd been broken to the saddle. Once he'd learned to bear my load, I could haul his ass back to the showers for a clean up so I could rim what I'd reamed.

He *was* more frantic than eager. His ass arched high; his legs locked tight around my chest and slowly worked their way down towards the small of my back. I planted my hands beside his armpits, dug my toes into the bed, shoved my dick hard against his tight marine pucker, and hovered above his face, memorizing every perfect preppy line. I'm not normally much of a thinker while I'm on the job; but even then, excited as I was, I knew that years hence I'd look back on Lance as one of the high points of my life. I wanted to remember every hair and pore, every twinkle and twinge so that whatever else life had in store for me, I'd have that night, always.

My slicked, throbbing dick pressed harder against his twitching, pink marine pucker, half psyching him out, half hoping to stretch the moment past forever. The slut parted his lips to echo the hunger that lived deep in his Bambi-brown eyes, but my swollen nine inches fucked him mute. His lips and lashes both clenched shut to meet the waves of pain I knew would be ripping his guts apart. I also knew when the muscles of his temple unknotted and his mouth gaped open to suck at the air, he felt *good* like a marine should.

One of the first jarheads I'd done while I was still in bootcamp explained how they felt. Some marines never go near dick, mainly because they're afraid they can't handle the strain. Only the hard-Corps jarheads need to prove themselves enough to risk everything from their asses to self-respect. Nobody wants to think he can't handle pain, but each of us has his limits. The first couple times a marine spreads wide, he just needs thick dick up his butt to prove to himself he is man enough to handle the pain he's heard so much about. Then, slowly, the more dick he does, the more he realizes how good that having his shithole stretched feels. Slutting becomes so habit-forming he isn't content unless he has swollen milkbone slammed up his slick shit-chute and pubes ground hard into the ruins of his fuckhole. My marine mentor confessed that most grunts stroke around all macho and trim on the outside, but empty as a politburo's promise on the inside. Only with their legs in the air and their shit-chutes stretched tight around thick dick slamming their guts to tapioca can they be happy. Even then, as soon as their butts are flushed full of jism and the meat of the minute is reclaimed, they start craving their next fuck-fix.

When Lance opened his eyes and looked up into mine, lost in the worshipful pleasure of the moment, I knew he hadn't put out in ages. My rod had rammed hard up into his tight foxhole in one swift, greedy, relentless stroke. Lance's muscles had seized up, but his slick hot marine guts latched around my lizard as though it were a holy relic. I'd lain still inside him for the moment it took his body to adjust to pleasure, but the dry heat of his guts swelled my meat deep within him and called me to action. His hands slipped back to polish my glutes like crystal balls that held his destiny. His hands and heels pulled me deeper into his ass until I was scratching at the twisted end of his fuck-tunnel buried nine inches up his need.

He moaned soft and low, shamelessly wallowing in the rare pleasure of being stretched tight around another man, yielding up his body in exchange for a few moments' peace. His spaniel-like gaze of devotion was so absolute I had to look away, half embarrassed, down to his parted lips and the strong jaw slackened by sensuality. My lips slipped to his shoulders and neck — and would have returned to his tits if he hadn't pinned me so tight in his cock-hungry clutches. As it was, I was able to lap at his neck, slurping up the remnants of the day's sweat-bred musk his sloppy shower had missed. Caught head and tail, his body shivered helplessly in pleasure as my lips moved to his left ear lobe and my tongue trilled beyond into the deepest secrets of his ear.

His moans had grown to grunts, but shivering and quivering though he was, the last thing the slut wanted was for me to stop. The arch of his ass proved that. His hole pressed tighter against my crotch, fucking himself even deeper up my dork, begging for more. Never one to give a bootcamp his way, I took back about seven inches of what I'd given him — and then slammed it back down through his ass with interest. If anything, his guts were greedier than ever, riffling along my rod like Nebraska wheat teasing the wind. I felt his massive mounds of marine manmuscle clamp shut along my shaft to hold me hostage. I pulled completely out again to teach his ass a lesson, popping his shithole like a balloon when my super-swollen dickhead flew through. Then I drilled deeper, angling hard against his prostate on the way past. Once more his body seized and shivered, but I had forgotten mercy. If he was going to sob and beg, it was time one marine asshole learned a few things about life.

My hips knew what to do. I turned them loose to slam my rapacious ramrod down where it belonged while I took stock of the hard male body that quivered below me. I felt my spine flex in and out, flying along in the breeder's arc evolution had taught our kind before we made it down from the trees. His hands had left my ass by now and were clamped tight around my shoulders, as though he were afraid I might remember something more important I had to do than keep fucking him hard up his tight marine ass. Well, at least it *had* been tight marine ass.

My eyes returned to his for a long moment before I ignored his need to breathe and slipped my Jackson lips against his, sucking gently at first and then using his mouth the way my dick was using his ass. The savage smack of my hips slamming against his upturned butt and driving dick deep enough to jar feral grunts from his parted preppy lips wove a hypnotic spell stronger than any opiate. If my marine was addicted to dick, I had already been seduced by the tight, masculine nature of his ass, I smelt his sweat and mine as they mingled in pools between his pecs and along his cobbled belly. The glorious stench of mansex thickened the air until our lean, hard bodies were thrusting and heaving together, lost awash in a sweet, stingless honeyed sea which threatened to pull us, unrepentant, into its lush, limpid, languorous depths.

One sensation blurred hopelessly into the next. A lifetime too soon, I felt my balls clench in a seizure of their own. I tried for an instant to hold back and knew there was no point. Lost, I picked up my speed, determined to teach his foxy bootcamp butt what real men feel like. He felt my Jackson jism jetting upwards, too; his hands clutched at my head, smearing my lips against his while my dick drilled deeper into the marine ass climbing to meat it. The taste and smell and sound of sex wrapped around us like a deafening cocoon; sensations were at once unbearable and inexpressible, deep enough to shatter the soul, yet ephemeral as perfect youth.

When my thick frothy load of seaman's semen blasted up into Lance's marine guts, I felt closer to him than any brother. His hands and feet clawed at my body, holding me tight against the world; but he was helpless against my own limitations. Fine as I felt humping his hole, feeling wave after prick-pulsing wave of spooge slam up through my dick to splatter off the deepest, most secret corners of his being, my pods eventually ran dry. Even then I didn't stop at once but slid on, snicker-snack through his hole to savor the slick texture of my load coating his ass and the spurts of spooge that sprayed back out to Spackle my thighs and balls with spent splatter. Eventually, though, I collapsed onto his chest and lay in his arms, only the bottom few inches of my crank still up his hole as though, like a bookmark, the end of my dick could remind me where I'd left off.

When I had recovered enough to think like a human again, I remembered his powerful Jackson joint. I ground my gut into his as I sucked at his lips, but wasn't able to tell whether the goo that bonded our bellies together was sweat or something more sinister. I've had more marines than I can count shoot off on their own, whether from the pressure on their prostates or the massive thrill of being juiced themselves. I needed to suck Lance's marine meat; but before I could open myself up to him, I needed to prove one last time who was in charge. He sighed a bit, accepting the inevitable, as I eased the rest of my rod out of his foxhole. I think he was surprised, though, when I turned about to straddle his chest, shoving my ass into his face with a harsh ''Lick my hole, marine.''

Marines do love to follow orders. His hands pried my glutes apart to give his nose and tongue free access to my virtue. He may not have gotten any lately, but Lance was no apprentice ass-lick. His tongue flew straight and true as a Tomahawk toward my pucker and the impact was just as dramatic. His warhead drilled deep through my hardened muscle while his bumpy blade flared outward, stretching my tight hole for maximum effect. Once he'd made himself at home, his preppy lips locked tight around my fuckhole and began sucking lightly, urging my pucker-lips up along his tongue. My hold on sanity slipped.

I ground my butt hard into his face and heard him snuffling up my ass, contented as a hog, dexterous as an anteater, and horny as any young Jackson should be. The whore had shot off while I was up his ass; great clumps of white threads were marooned now on his chest and belly, drying as his sweat evaporated into the chilly, processed air of the room. The way his tongue was tearing into my tush told me I could get a piece of him at last. I sat harder onto his face, feeling my nuts droop down across his chin, as I reached down to pull up on his knees and bring his balls into range. I started on his 'nads to make sure they were cranking out another load. My tongue slid deep between his thighs and balls, licking clean his musky scent and, finally, slurping one nut at a time into my mouth for some serious ball-handling.

Lance seemed hardly to notice when I moved down to his crank, licking along his shaft, stripping it clean of its pearly load of old pre-cum and fresh jism salted with mansweat. The tongue-lashing he was giving my shithole was almost enough to make me forget this ten inches of marine weapon — almost. I had to pry the fucker out of the goo that coated his belly; but once I was able to look him in the face, I was more than ready to suck serious dick.

My lips slid swiftly across the hot, purple head of his dick. My mouth was watering a Niagara so slathering spit across his head to slick my way was no problem at all. Once I had his snout between my lips, his hips reacted, arching upward to slide more of what he had into my face. His tongue still twirled away up my asshole, but Lance was marine enough to handle two things at once.

My lips locked behind the pulsing trigger-ridge of his plum-sized head; my tongue tore into overdrive, slicing across his super-tender tool until moans and grunts joined the contented snuffles rising, muffled, from my ass. I slipped my suction up past MAX and eased my face even farther down his dork until, almost before I knew it, I'd used the curve in his stiff dick to match the curve in my throat and lock his Jackson dick down my gullet. I twisted this way along his shaft and pumped that. My chin ground into his golden pubes as though I could massage another load of marine cream up from his balls.

Between my butt and throat, Lance was getting more fun than any young marine deserves to have on liberty. We'd been deployed long enough, even after spunking with me up his ass, the slut didn't take long to prime his pump for another gusher. My fingers slid down to the mire up his asscrack to massage his butthole while I worked. Almost immediately, I saw his nuts rise into view and knew what was coming. Just in time, I jerked my jaw off his joint far enough for his massive meaty head to pop out again into my mouth. My tongue was on it like wasps on a company picnic the whole time my suction was slurping up his sweet, cream marine load.

Lance let loose an ancient scream of ecstasy bred to triumph as his body seized up even more solid. I slammed three fingers far up his shithole to tickle his gizzard and his fancy at once. That's where I stayed, splayed out inside him, pulling down with my paw and stretching his spooge-packed butt as I sucked upwards with my mouth, pulling the long, pearly ropes of more Jacksonian jism up from his nuts. For a moment, the lazy bootcamp slut was too busy having a good time to keep tonguing me up the hole. I slammed my ass back against his mouth and gave him something more to think about.

What with relishing the feel of his tongue up my ass and the taste of his load rolling across my tongue and the hot, creamy texture of his mouthorgan, I was one busy surface warrior. Fortunately, Lance was an even busier desert defender. I'll never know how long I spent sucking wad after glorious jarhead wad out of his swollen dick. I know long after he ran dry, I kept up the pressure. I had to. That magical tongue up my ass dropped me into brainlock so complete that my entire being seemed bound up with the raw, tingling nerves of my asshole. Now and again I would feel his nose on my cheeks or more of my jism leak out into my hand, but I rocked and wriggled and squirmed about on the end of his butt-licker until half past forever. When his jaw finally locked up and I snapped back into the world enough to ease my face off his crank and unhand his hole, I collapsd atop him. Now it was his turn to hold me awhile before I taught him what a Jackson buttfuck would feel like once the pressure was off my balls and I could take my time. He held me tight against him, the sweat and jism drying on our bodies, until I pulled his ass back into the shower to prep it for Round II. During the rest of that night and the days that followed, we continued the match, ringing chimes to end round after round of brutal, heroic, glorious fucking without ever coming to the final bell. The next day we found a cheaper room so we could stay off the ship until it pulled out to await developments. Most of the marines aboard were pissed they never got to storm ashore to liberate Kuwait. I see their point. They've probably missed being involved in *the* war of their generation by just a few miles. Lance and I weren't bored during the long spring months that followed as we floated about the Gulf waiting for history to happen. We were busy finding new gear lockers and fan rooms and other out-of-the-way places to tend to business. It wasn't the business of making war; but by the time we sailed back east to the States, we were the best-trained pair of buddy-fuckers in US military history.

BLACKBALLED!

WILLIAM COZAD

W HEN GREYHOUND WENT ON STRIKE I had to take the commuter train to and from work. It was a different experience, riding the rails. Most people read the newspaper or snooze. But I just looked out the window.

I daydreamed a lot to forget about my boring job. Most often I fantasized about guys I saw on the street or on the train, guys going home to families in the suburbs. Because I'm single, I could move to the city. But I like my big apartment and don't want to swap it for a cheap residence hotel in the city.

One day I did some shopping after work. I needed more shorts and socks since I change them every day and they don't last forever. But I ended up missing my usual train and had to take a later one.

The train wasn't jammed like it usually is. Seated by himself was a young black sailor. I thought he was sort of interesting looking, what with his Navy uniform and sailor cap. Although there were plenty of empty seats I plopped down right next to him.

I think he was sort of surprised. Since he had a newspaper on his lap, I figured he was probably dozing. I gave him a quick smile. Then he nodded and closed his eyes. I thought maybe he'd want to talk. But since I'm not much of a conversationalist, I was content just to sit next to the handsome black man.

The train roared along. While he was catnapping I got a good look at him. Smooth features. Trim mustache over his thick luscious lips. Somewhere in his early twenties.

He was seated next to the window so I could pretend to be looking at the view in case he caught me checking him out. There were a couple of other passengers seated nearby but luckily they weren't paying any attention to us.

Looking at the black sailor gave me a hard-on. My cock pulsed and I squeezed it. I've always thought sailors are the cream of the crop of American manhood. Young, healthy guys. Red-blooded and horny. I'd had my share of them in my younger days and I'd always tended to like the blond ones best. But now I prefer men of color.

Back in college I'd lusted after a black football player. He was real muscular and he always sweated a lot. I fantasized about slurping up his sweat and his cock too while I was at it. Like Martin Luther King, I had a dream. But it never came to pass. Harry was nice and friendly but I never had the nerve to make a move on him. He didn't have a clue about what I wanted even though I obsessively cruised him. So I had to content myself by whacking off and fantasizing about the black hunk.

Now I was seated beside a handsome Afro-American sailor. I wanted to look at his crotch but it was covered by a newspaper. With any luck maybe it would fall off. Or maybe I could move it aside. Or maybe I'd be better off to mind my own business, I decided.

But no harm in looking at the black sailor. Ebony skin. Smooth, muscular body. About average height. Bet he packed a big black rod. They say black dicks are bigger. And as proof, a guy who'd spent years as a corpsman in the Navy once told me he'd looked at hundreds of dicks over the years and said the black ones were definitely bigger on the average by at least two inches.

Like some people on the train probably thought about what they were going to have for dinner at night, I thought about what I was going to jack-off over. Tonight I knew what it was going to be: that hunky black sailor boy.

My cock was not only hard but it was also oozing pre-cum. Little wonder why I was so horny! I even thought about ducking into the toilet and pulling my prick. But I decided it would be better to wait and take a leisurely bath, soap up and jerk off, spewing my wad on the water.

At first I thought I was dreaming when I felt the black sailor's leg brush against mine. Maybe it was just due to the movement of the train. Besides, he was probably asleep, but I decided to apply a little pressure from my leg against his. Then my boner suddenly lurched in my pants.

Maybe he was dreaming. I hoped he didn't wake up right away. His fingers touched my thigh, accidentally of course. I watched him. Eyes closed but breathing even. Asleep. Or *was* he? When I put my hand on his, he didn't move it away.

By then I was breathing more heavily. I wanted to reach under that newspaper that covered his lap and grab a handful of his goodies. But I wasn't that brazen. And besides that, I didn't want a fight on my hands. This could have all been accidental, wishful thinking on my part. So I decided to cool it.

Leaning back in the seat, I folded my hands over my cock, partly to conceal its hardness from the conductor who roamed up the aisle, partly because it felt good to hold my own.

All of a sudden the newspaper sort of shifted over onto my lap. I thought I was imagining things. But out of the corner of my eye I looked at that bulge in the sailor's crotch. There was the outline of a big snake coiled inside the flap and you could see the mushroom shape of the cockhead. The sailor had sprung a boner, sure as shit!

His hand crept under the newspaper, moved mine away and grabbed hold of my cock. I thought I'd cream my pants! The next thing I knew, the sailor had unzipped the fly and grasped hold of my meat. First he jacked it slowly. Then that hot black hand tightened around my cock and made it ooze all the more.

"Let me see yours," I said.

Though the sailor spread out the newspaper to cover both our laps I didn't know if our crotches were out of the field of vision of the other passengers or not. At this point that wasn't my main concern. What interested me more was the fact that he had unbuttoned the thirteen buttons of his flap and his hard cock was poking the newspaper like a tent pole.

Peeking under the paper, I saw a huge black trouser-snake — easily nine, maybe ten inches long. And *thick*. With a pink head and a slit that drooled clear goo. I grabbed that cock and choked it, feeling its head and power. Then, under the cover of the paper, the sailor and I pumped each other's prick.

Looking out the window, I realized that I was close to my stop. Maybe the conductor would check my ticket again and put me off. He was moving down the aisle and it certainly wouldn't have done for him to have caught on to what we were doing.

We both got our horses back in the barn in the nick of time, the newpaper discreetly covering the sailor's lap by the time the conductor passed by.

"This is my stop."

"Aw, shit," he sighed.

"Can you get off with me?"

"My family's expecting me."

"Fuck!"

"I could phone and say I'll be late."

"Great."

I got off the train downtown with the sailor. He made a quick call. Then we walked the mile to my place.

"Man, I got a real case of blue balls," the sailor said.

"I'll take care of that."

"How much farther is it?"

"Keep walking. It'll be worth it, like walking a mile for a Camel."

"I don't smoke," he said.

"I just suck."

"We'll see about that."

Once inside my digs the sailor was all over me. I felt that big black cock poking against my belly and my own cock was pressing against his. Then when I took off his white hat, I discovered that his hair was cut real short, making him look even younger than he had at first glance.

"How old are you?"

"Twenty-four."

"Don't look it."

"That's what everybody says."

With those words, the sailor then went for my neck, sucking it and giving me a hickey while I squeezed his buns. Though I was going to offer him a drink, we were both too hungry for each other to be bothered with cocktails. Standing beside the bed, both of us stripped. And I quickly found out that that monster cock of his looked even bigger than it felt.

Suddenly the sailor pushed me down and covered me with his hot black body. No doubt he was a real lover. When his lips touched mine, I felt the tickle of his mustache. Then my lips parted and his tongue probed my mouth.

He licked all over my body, down to my towering prick. When his lips encircled it I felt his hot, wet mouth mold around my cockhead. Then he engulfed the entire shaft.

I couldn't wait to get at his big black dick. Sure, I wanted him to suck me. But I also wanted to swing on that big black dick. Curling into a sixty-nine position, I faced the biggest, blackest cock of my life. First I held it and felt its pulse. Then, slurping on the cockhead, I sampled some pre-cum and went down on his thick shaft.

"Oh yeah, baby. Suck my big black dick. Take it all. You can do it. Show me that you love it." he exclaimed between slurps.

It took some doing but I was determined to prove to this sailor that I could handle his big black cock, taking all of it down my throat. I literally gobbled up the huge fucker!

"Oh baby, that's good. Suck it! Feels so good," he said.

Letting go of that black dick before it choked me to death, I started to jack it, frigging the skin up and down its deeply-veined ebony shaft. Then I licked his balls.

"Oh yeah, baby. Suck those balls, Get'm all wet and ready to blast. They're full of fucking jizz, just for you!"

The sailor went back to sucking my cock. I did the same, sealing my lips around his fuckstick and devouring it down my throat. Both of our rods were steely hard. Mine in his gullet, his in my mouth with my hand clasped firmly on the massive shaft, sucking the bloated cockhead, tasting the bubbling pre-cum.

With my mouth stuffed full of black cock, I let out a moan and spewed hot jizz down the sailor's throat. When he drank every drop of my load, it only endeared him to me all the more.

Taking his mouth off my meat, he suddenly rammed that mighty black rod down my throat. I held onto the shaft for dear life. But it was clear that there was no stopping him, no holding back his load. Gobs of the thickest cum I could ever remember filled my mouth. Then I swallowed every drop of the syrupy jism.

"Oh God, you shoot a mean load," I said.

"That was only the first one."

"What do you mean?"

"You'll see."

I swear that black dick didn't soften a bit. It throbbed and danced around with those big dangling low-hangers. Then the sailor crawled between my legs — with me on my back — and he began fisting the big dick to make it even harder.

"What are you going to do?"

"Exactly what you want me to do; I'm gonna give you a sample of black power."

"It's so big. I can't take it. Be merciful. Let me try to sit on it."

"Nope. I fuck my babies face-to-face. That way I can watch you scream and beg for more."

"Oh wow, I don't know."

Sure I wanted to be fucked by the black sailor. How often do you get to be hosed by such a monster of a cock?

The sailor just spat into my crack for lube. But he was also drooling lots of pre-cum which made the entry more endurable. An inch at a time, I could feel it penetrate me.

His strong black arms held my torso while he spread my asshole. With his meat stuffed inside me he started to thrust his hips.

"Fuck me, you black devil. I want that big dick, *all* of it," I cried.

The sailor grinned while he pumped my hole, building up a fire in my ass like I hadn't felt for years. Fucking slow and deep at first, he then picked up the pace until he was slamming into my ass like a wild man. His cock was hard as coal and it rammed inside me until his nuts exploded, spraying my assguts with his hot black sailor jizz.

Scissoring my legs around his black ass, I held onto him as my ass muscles spasmed. Then I felt my cum ooze onto his belly, signaling that he'd gotten me off while fucking me — something I don't ever remember having happened before.

Travis, that was his name, drank a Coke while I guzzled a cold beer. We stayed naked, taking some slides on each other's meat. But mostly we just kissed and hugged.

"I lied to you about something," he said, lightly strumming a finger across my well-fucked b-hole.

"About what? You're a real sailor, aren't you? I know you're really black. What?"

It occurred to me that there might be some trouble. Maybe he wanted money or something. Maybe he couldn't handle the fact that he was gay. Maybe he'd freak and try to hurt me.

"That business about my family. . . . See, I got a sugar daddy, lover, whatever. He's real jealous. So we can't see each other again. Dig?"

"Sure. Whatever you say."

I'd had hopes of his staying the night. Maybe we'd even end up having regular suck and fuck sessions. Who knows what. But my hopes were instantly dashed.

"You're a nice guy. I really like you. But I got me a baby and I go to sleep in his arms every night. He knows I play around some because I'm still young. But he loves me, takes good care of me. When I get out of the Navy in a few months we're going to live together."

"He's a lucky guy to have you."

"That's what I tell him," the sailor cracked a grin. Then Travis gave me a big kiss and hug, saying that perhaps it would be best if he were to walk back to the train by himself.

THE FRENCH SAILOR

WILLIAM COZAD

I ALWAYS THOUGHT the best-looking boys in the world were in the navy, especially the American sailors. They tend to be fresh, young and horny. But I also liked to check out the *foreign* sailors when they visited the port of San Francisco.

I can vividly recall a ship from Turkey, its crew being trained in maneuvers by our navy. The stout, dark young men always hung around on lower Mission Street, near the bus terminal — looking for sex — and gay men used to pick them up in cars. The sailors weren't too good-looking for the most part, but they *were* randy. *I* certainly made it with one — nothing memorable except that the swabbie rubbed his crotch to signal his desires since he didn't speak English.

The most recent navy ship to visit our city was the *Jeanne d'Arc* from France. On Market Street I took a look at the crew. Some were dark and some were fair. But without exception, they were the best-looking boys I'd seen in a long time.

I spotted four of them in front of a movie theater. One was a blond, blue-eyed boy in his early twenties. I fell in love with him at first sight when I smiled at him and he smiled back. I thought the romance was over when his buddies went to the ticket window. But luck had it that only three of them went into the theater — while the blond hunk stayed outside.

"How do you like San Francisco?" I asked.

"A beautiful city," he replied with a heavy, nasal accent.

Although I'd never seen Paris or any other city out of the States, that's what tourists *always* said about San Francisco. So much for small talk; I decided it was time to make my move. More than one passing gay guy took a look at me talking to the French sailor. And if I didn't get him soon, someone *else* would sure try to!

"You can walk everywhere," the sailor observed, presenting me with a perfect opportunity to lure him off the street.

"How would you like to go for a drink? You like American beer?" I suggested.

"Oui," he nodded.

His wee-wee was definitely on my mind . . . and I was hoping it was a big one!

"What's your name?" I asked, cutting one eye toward his fat crotch.

"Pierre. Peter in English." An ironic smile flicked across his lips.

"Have you seen much of the city?"

"Fisherman's Wharf, Chinatown, Coit Tower, even rode the cable car."

No need to waste a lot of time with the tourist sites bit, I figured. Getting in my car, I drove him directly to my place, a house above Army Street that had a view of downtown. It also had a balcony which linked my house with that of my neighbor, Ken. Since we were also good friends, we often shared tricks. We both liked young military types. More than once we'd sent one of these studs across the balcony to the other's bedroom! *That*, however, was not information I shared with Pierre when I took him out on the balcony.

He marveled at the panoramic view of the downtown area with Market Street and all its twinkling lights. But soon I steered him back into the living room and served Pierre the frosty bottle of Miller beer which I'd promised earlier.

"We drink wine with our meals aboard ship," he commented.

No wonder Frenchmen had an alcoholism rate about quadruple that of the United States, I inwardly speculated. Then, when I looked over at Pierre, I decided that if I didn't know differently, I'd've guessed that my French guest was too young to be served a drink in the U.S. Though I'd seen his Naval I.D. — and it proved that he was twenty-two — Pierre looked like a youngster in his sailor suit.

A white hat with a red pom-pom on top and a picture of Jeanne d'Arc on the headband framed his smooth-shaven face. And a dark blue suit with a striped shirt covered his slender frame. Naturally, I wanted to see what awaited underneath. So to get the ball rolling, I popped a cassette into the VCR and waited for his reaction to seeing a good old-fashioned fuck-film. Soon enough, I detected a bulge in his crotch. And when I groped him, I discovered that his cock was rock-hard!

Slowly I undressed him, taking off his shoes and socks, his jumper and uniform pants. His body was smooth and creamy-white, with small pink nipples capping his chest. It was understandable why I went to work with my tongue, taking him on a trip around the world. Nuzzling his pits, swabbing my tongue across his chest, sucking on his nipples until they were hard, I sampled the top half of his beautiful body. Then, when I scooted down between his legs, I noticed that his briefs were tented with a hard-on! To tease him however, I licked his inner thighs and his shins — even sucked his toes and lapped between them — until he was breathing heavily and moaning in a plaintive, nasal tone.

Putting my hands in the waistband of his shorts, I pulled them down, revealing his blond bush and engorged uncut cock, its rosy head peeking out of the sheath and *drooling* pre-cum. I shucked off my clothes and put my arms around him. ''Oh Pierre, you're beautiful. Beautiful French sailor boy,'' I whispered, stroking his satin-smooth back.

He smiled. His lips were ruby and pouty. I kissed them and they kissed back. I licked between them and probed his mouth while I grabbed hold of his fiery fuckmeat and rubbed the satiny flap of skin over the flared head that dripped goo.

Crawling between his legs, I held his shaft while I licked the spongy, flared pink cockhead. I could taste the aged cheese and the salty pre-cum. Holding the head, I flicked my tongue across the alabaster shaft. Then I slowly jacked the skin of the shaft over the head while I licked his balls.

He responded with a deep moan while I sucked on his balls. Managing to snake around into a sixty-nine position, I confronted him with my own randy prick. He held it and jacked it slowly as though he had not had any previous experience in mansex.

His cock was throbbing when I took it in my mouth and sucked on its rubbery hardness. After I deep-throated it down to his balls — my nose buried in his pubes — I tried to get him to suck me. But he didn't understand what I'd asked him — or didn't *want* to.

That was all right because I was determined to suck him off so good that it would give new meaning to Franco-American relations. Kneeling between his legs, I spread them. His hairless ass-crack and its pink, puckered hole looked so tasty that I couldn't resist diving between his legs and lapping at his crack. I don't think he expected that, but he writhed on the sofa while I did it. Locating the puckered hole, I darted into it and tongue-fucked it to my heart's content.

But sailor or not, his interest in the tingling, wet sensation I was giving him led me to believe that Pierre would not object if I were to explore further with bigger and harder objects. That had been my experience. And simply looking at him made me all the hotter to do the naughty things I had in mind. His misty blue eyes invited me straight to his gorgeous ass. But not wanting to ignore his towering stiff prick, I put my mouth around it again. Then I suddenly discovered that if I lifted his smooth ass-globes up a little, I could nudge his asscrack with my own drooling prick while I sucked his cock!

With no protests from him, I managed to rub my cock into his crack. Gently but forcefully, I pushed past his assring and my cockhead slipped into his cherry, tight fuckhole. My probing cock soon stretched the hole. Then my shaft slithered inside the furnace of his body.

He bit his lower lip and groaned but made no effort to stop my advances or push me out of him. While I entrenched my boner inside him, I wrapped my fingers around his pulsing prick and jacked it.

With only slight maneuvering, I discovered that I could bend down and take the flared uncut head of his cock in my mouth while, at the same time, keeping my own cockhead ensconced in his hot hole.

In the manner of a derrick drilling on an oil field, I sucked on his cock while I fucked his ass. This was certainly a first for me! Though I'd been in three-ways where I'd blown one guy and plowed another at the same time, I could never remember doing both things to the same guy! I'd *heard* that it was possible. But until Pierre came along, I'd never even bothered to try it.

Maybe it took special guys to do special things to. I could even *deep-throat* Pierre while I pulled my prick nearly out of his ass, practically letting go of his cock while I thrust deep inside him! He encouraged me with some French words that sounded really dirty. Then he rubbed my head, pulling at my hair until tears stung my eyes.

I kept sucking him, adding pressure to his sensitive crown, tonguing under its ridge and gobbling up his shaft. His cock got harder and harder and he thrust it deep into my throat. He grunted and I felt the cream jettison out of his nuts and spew into my mouth. I kept my lips clamped tightly around his cock.

Tasting his rich cream in my mouth took me over the edge. With his manjuice guzzling down my gullet, I rammed my cock home — deep into the bowels of the French sailor. My balls slapped his tender asscheeks and exploded their load, spraying the walls of his insides, coating them with American cum. I stayed still until my cock softened slightly and slithered out of the tight, deflowered French-boy butthole. Then I spit his cock out of my mouth.

I don't know what made me do it but I crawled on top of his chest and rubbed my cock against those pouty, ruby lips. As I rubbed it against his cheeks, wiping the cum and assjuices into his face, his lips parted.

His mouth was hot and wet, like his asshole. And after he had cleaned off my cock, tasting the exotic mixture in his mouth, he nursed my boner until it went soft. Then Pierre put his unifrom on.

We went back onto the balcony and drank another beer. I gave him my address and drove him back to the *Jeanne d'Arc*, docked at the Embarcadero. Then, when I got home, my neighbor Ken was waiting for me.

"You look like you had a wild night," he slyly observed.

"I *did* . . . with a gorgeous young French sailor! Hottest sex I ever had," I bragged.

"I *know*." Ken smiled.

Then he confessed to me that he had heard a lot of moaning and groaning and had gone out onto the balcony to check up on me. When he'd seen me suck and fuck Pierre at the same time, Ken had jacked off twice while watching us. At least that's what he *told* me!

NIGHT BUS TO RENO

WILLIAM COZAD

I WAS BORED. I needed a change of scenery, a getaway. That's why I took the night bus to Reno.

I wouldn't get there until the wee hours, but that didn't matter. Reno is an around-the-clock city for gambling and drinking. I'm not much for either, although I don't mind trying my luck occasionally. I don't mind a few beers now and then, either.

I didn't need an excuse to lose. My life fell apart after my ex-lover split. But I thought about that shit-kicker song that said thank God and the Greyhound he's gone.

Now I was on the Greyhound myself. I located a seat next to a sleepy young man. I nodded at him and he gave me a little smile and closed his eyes.

The bus groaned along in the night. With the overhead light on in front of me I got a good look at the young man. He was handsome with his black hair cut high and tight and long lashes closed over his brown eyes. He was wearing a blue nylon racing jacket, a T-shirt, blue denims and white Reeboks. His head was cradled against the window.

As the bus crossed the Sierras it turned and tossed the young man against me. His leg touched mine and his head fell on my shoulder. I had to be dreaming. I felt my cock stir.

Looking down at his crotch, I noted the big bulge, but there was no outline of his equipment.

I felt the urge to grope him but refrained. I didn't need a fight, and I certainly didn't need to get thrown off the bus in the middle of nowhere. But I could look, that was no harm. His hands were locked between his thighs just below his basket.

The bus climbed the summit, which was seven thousand feet, and then descended into the Reno valley, lurching on the turns in the road. I lost all track of time.

The young man awoke and rubbed the sleep out of his eyes. "Are we almost there?" he asked.

"Won't be long now."

He looked around like a sleepy boy, hardly old enough to gamble. Maybe he was just going to visit someone.

"Been here before?" he asked.

"Many times."

"This is my first time."

"They take your money, old or new."

He sort of smiled.

"Well, I don't have all that much."

"You don't look old enough for casinos or bars."

"I'm twenty-one. Just got out of boot camp."

"You're a soldier?"

"Uh-huh. U.S. Government property, like they say."

He reached under his T-shirt and dangled his dog tags.

"I'll be —" Boy, was that a surprise. A healthy young soldier in his prime. Handsome, recruiting poster-type kid.

The skyline of Reno was visible, the casinos and all the lights of what was called the biggest little city in the world.

My cock stayed semi-hard. I liked military men but it had been ages since I'd had any of Uncle Sam's prime beef. He was a young, red-blooded all-American boy and had to be horny. I had to be dreaming that I'd get my meat hooks on him.

The bus entered Reno with its garish lights and people in the streets with drinks in their hands. It stopped at the Hilton and a few people got off.

I took another look at the young soldier. He flashed me a toothy smile with perfect white teeth.

"I don't know where to go in Reno," he said.

"You could tag along with me it you like. What kind of gambling do you like, cards, dice?"

"Naw, I just want to play the slots."

"Harrah's are the most liberal, they say."

The bus stopped at Harrah's and we got off together.

"Lot of bright lights."

"They can afford it."

Inside the casino I got my cash, food and drink refund for my bus ticket coupon.

"I don't have the casino ticket. I'm going back home to Salt Like."

"Where are you stationed?"

"Basic at Fort Ord. But I'm going to paratrooper training at Fort Benning, Georgia."

"Jump out of planes?"

"I've always wanted to be a paratrooper. My father was one. My friends back home think I'm crazy but the Army trains you to do that."

At the bar I got us each a beer with my coupon.

"Thanks. I'm Richard."

"Bill." I thought I should say William, but no one ever called me that except my ex-lover when he was mad.

"Pleased to meet you."

"My pleasure. Richard, not Dick?"

"Everyone calls me Richard."

Richard roamed along the banks of slot machines and pulled the handles. He didn't win anything big but got enough coins back to keep playing.

"Pull the handle. Try your luck," he encouraged.

He put in the quarter and I yanked the handle. Got a cherry and two coins for one.

"Too slow for me," I said.

"Yeah? What do you like to play?"

"Craps. That's fast action. Better odds. But I don't gamble seriously anymore. I just like to drink some beer and look around."

Richard played some multiple coin machines and didn't have much luck.

"Guess I'd better go to the bus depot. I can sleep there until my bus leaves for Salt Lake."

"When's that?"

"0800."

"That's hours away. Here, let me give you some more quarters."

"No, that's okay."

"You can play for both of us, partners."

"Well . . . you sure?"

"Yeah, go ahead."

I bought him a couple of rolls of quarters and he played the slots. The cocktail waitress brought us some free beer (free except that they cost twenty bucks apiece considering what we lost between us). Richard's machine kept sucking up the quarters.

He was down to four quarters when he pulled the handle and three swamis lined up, a red light went on and an alarm siren sounded. The machine dropped several coins and the attendant verified the jackpot and paid the balance of seventy-five dollars.

Richard insisted on splitting it with me, even though I refused.

"It's your luck," I said.

"Yeah, but your money, partner."

"Why don't we get a room. You can snooze until your bus leaves. I'll pay for it with my half."

"I'll buy the booze."

Richard bought a bottle of Seagram's whiskey and a twelve-pack of Budweiser at an all-night store and I led him through the alleys to a place on Lake Street. They have rooms with views of the cascading lights on the Circus Circus casino at night and the snow-capped mountains in the daytime.

Richard had his luggage checked through to Salt Lake where he would be staying on leave.

"The Mormons used to own this hotel, but they sold it to a group of investors," I said.

"I'm not a Mormon. But some of my relatives are," he said.

In a large room on the tenth floor with the view of Reno we drank boilermakers, his favorite, whiskey chased down with beer.

"I'd like to take a shower," he said.

"Sure. Go ahead."

I turned on the radio station to some soft music, sipped beer and looked at the view. I could hear the sound of the shower and wondered what Richard looked like nude.

He took a long time but he came out with a towel cinched around his waist and his body beaded with water. His body was hard and hairless. He was like a wet dream.

"Guess I'd better catch some z's. Wake me in a couple hours, okay?"

"Sure. I'll just drink your booze and enjoy the view."

"That's what it's for."

Was he talking about the view outside the room, or inside?

Richard lay on the sheet without covers and the towel fell off his waist. He was incredibly beautiful, with a big uncut cock that lay over big balls. When he turned over his ass was sculpted and hairless. I wanted to jack-off looking at him. He was wearing only his metal dog tags on the chain around his neck.

When he turned over again his cock was hard and pointing skyward. I couldn't help it. I had to touch it. He was sawing logs.

I sat down on the edge of the bed. Maybe the courage came from the booze but I wrapped my fingers around his cock. He opened his eyes.

"Oh man, I didn't think you were like that."

"I'm sorry, Richard. You're just so gorgeous."

"No, I mean that's why I jacked off in the shower."

"You've got a big dick."

"Go ahead, beat it."

He gave me permission to masturbate him. Well, my own cock was raging in my pants. I stripped naked.

I got between Richard's legs and held my hard cock against his and stroked them together. Next thing I knew he took over jacking my cock with his left hand while he jacked his own with his right hand.

"Oh, beat it baby. Beat your meat for me."

I gently moved his hand away and took over whacking off myself. I could get the stroke better. I was real hot but I wanted to see him shoot off first.

The horny young soldier fisted his eight-incher with the overhang. It towered stiff and straight, a cock of rare beauty.

"Shoot it, soldier. Shoot that big load!"

He was used to taking orders and he blew. Three, no, four big geysers of jizz like Old Faithful shot all over the place.

Seeing his pearly joy-juice splattered all over his belly, I knew that I'd blast pronto. I tugged on my cock and grunted. Gobs of creamy jism gushed out of my pee hole.

I lay down on the bed beside Richard. I wanted to put my arms around him and kiss him but I didn't want him to freak out.

"I ain't never done nothing with another man before. But I thought about it a lot, wondered what it would be like."

"What did you do before you joined the Army?"

"Worked in a gas station and chased pussy. But that wasn't what I wanted, not really. Besides, the Army will pay for my college later."

"Young men need time to find their way. Want another drink?"

"No, I just want to lay here with you. I laid against you on the bus because of the way you looked at me. When you didn't touch me I figured you weren't interested."

"Now you know better."

He turned over on his side and backed his ass against my cock.

"You're going to get me going again," I said.

"Good, that's what I want."

If I got the vibrations right, he wanted me to fuck his cherry soldier butt. I'd kill to get a hot ass like his.

I rubbed his back and his buttcheeks. They were firm and muscular. I'm an ass man, always have been. Sucking cock is only an appetizer for me. Fucking ass is the main course.

His asscrack was steamy when I probed it, and hairy. I fingered his tight little hole.

"Do it, man. Screw me."

He rolled over on his belly. I guess he'd thought about doing this before, because he wanted it, I could tell.

I had a small tube of K-Y and rubbers I kept in my jacket pocket just in case I got lucky.

You could have all the chips in Reno for all I cared now. I was getting a cherry soldier boy and that was priceless to me.

I lubed his kiester and threaded a condom on my cock. His asshole was really tight and I had quite a time opening him up. I know it hurt him at first. But I tried to be as gentle as I could.

Once my cock was embedded in his butt-hole he began moaning and panting and moving his ass around.

"Fuck me," he whispered. "Fuck my ass!"

He made little sighs of delight as I pumped his hole. The sighs got louder and turned into squeals. His assmuscles gripped my cock. It had been ages since I'd fucked such a hot, tight ass, and even longer since I'd deflowered a young guy.

He wanted it bad, though, the way he shoved back. He was a natural ass-fucker, took to it like a duck to water.

"Do it, man. Shoot that load of cum up my ass. Fill that fucking scumbag."

He was begging for it, but I didn't let him rush me. I wanted to take my time, feeling all those nooks and crannies of his asshole through the latex sheath on my cock.

"Oh shit, it's so hard. It's gonna shoot. Oh fuck, I can feel it!"

I blasted wads of scalding jizz into his rubber-lined shithole.
"Feels so fucking good! Bag of hot cum up my asshole!"
I pulled my cock out of him, with the rubber intact.
"Got another rubber?"
"Sure."
He rolled over on his back and his cock was stiff and throbbing.
"Put it on my dick, okay?"
I rubberized his cock.
"Grease up your asshole."
I lubed my crack.
"Now sit on my cock, man."
The soldier gave the orders and I obeyed him, impaling my ass on his fat uncut cock.

He must have fucked a lot of girls this way, riding the peg, because he thrust while I bounced my ass up and down on his soldier cock.

"Aw fuck, it's cumming! Take my cum up your fucking ass."
I felt the hot load spew into my rubber-lined assguts. I slowly moved my ass off his cock. He was young but all stud, this soldier. I knew that I'd been fucked by a real man.

I bent down and kissed him on the mouth. I know most guys don't like that at first with another man but he didn't object. We even swapped some spit.

Richard got dressed and I walked to the bus station with him and put him on the bus. He wanted my address and phone number and I gave it to him, thinking I'd never see him again.

I crawled around the green felt jungles of the casinos and tossed the dice and played blackjack. I sipped some beer. I didn't win and I didn't lose, just sort of broke even.

On the bus ride home that night I thought of Richard the soldier and my cock stayed stiff all the way home. I didn't think I'd ever see him again but I've gotten lucky before.

Out of the blue the letter from him came a couple of weeks later. He had bad luck in the paratrooper training and broke a leg. He was okay otherwise but couldn't complete the training and was being transferred back to the infantry at Fort Ord. He wanted to see me again.

It was an unlucky break for him, I guess, but I felt like I had finally hit the jackpot.

HARD TO THE CORPS

BRAD HENDERSON, USMC

I COULD TELL YOU about the first time I saw Keith standing lined up with the rest of us recruits in bootcamp. I could talk of watching him shower or marching beside me. I could even tell you how I finally managed to get him shitfaced enough to put the moves on him. You're probably more interested in the way that thick pre-cum of his pooled clear and pure inside the oversized foreskin that covered his huge marine dick as it finally stiffened up for me. You'll want to know how pumped his tight marine body looked stretched out on the bed as I climbed between those strong thighs and slid my mouth far enough open to work him inside. Most of all, you'll want to know how that huge, delicious cock tasted that night years ago.

I knew he wasn't nearly as drunk as he pretended, but I understood. By then I knew he wanted the same thing I did. He just didn't know how to admit his needs to himself. Ever since that first day of bootcamp, I had been able to think of nothing but that huge slab of meat swinging between his legs and the powerful butt that hung hard and ready for action behind his hips, full of magic and just waiting for my best asset to part him open. Marines come in two basic flavors: cute and bestial. Keith isn't the butch killer type; he's the model of the perfectly built Iowa boy next door who goes off to join the Corps and defend freedom — with the face of Tom Harmon, the body of Chris Reeves, and the politics of Sergeant York. Those green eyes and that pug nose, his Hollywood-style teeth and powerful, hairless pecs all combined together to keep my heart racing. Then that uncut marvel swung into my life and I was in love.

When I was finally able to have my way with him, I didn't know where to start. He's 6'3'' and built, so just getting his clothes off him wasn't easy. When I got his sneakers off, though, and smelt his scent, I'd have done anything for sex. His jeans and t-shirt didn't stand a chance. He lay still while I licked like a spaniel at the insides of his thighs. They were covered in blond hair so fine that it was almost invisible. Working my way up

Keith's hard, tanned thighs, I parked myself at his balls and nudged them first with my nose, filling my lungs with his man-scent. By the time I'd rooted his ballbag aside and shoved my face clear up into his crotch, I was able to fill my lungs with one perfect lungful after another. Bred of his sweat and musk and the other delicious remains of his day, that glorious man-scent was unlike anything I'd ever dreamed possible. Even the stench of our beers on his skin turned me on until I was lapping at his crotch and balls like a whore. His hairy balls mocked me, retreating when I tried to give them the tongue-lashing they deserved so I sucked them inside my mouth, rolling them around my tongue and squeezing them gently between my teeth. As I lifted my face away from his crotch, pulling his balls tight in my mouth, I saw the idea of castration flicker across his face before he smiled and said something about my not wanting to destroy his cum-factory. I'd had temporarily enough of those huge balls by that time any-way and had to decide about my next step. I could follow the scent of his musk to lick that classic marine ass of his until it was as spit-shined as his shoes. I caught a glance of that pre-cum over-flowing his cock, drizzling down his crankshaft and then drool-ing in long, thin strands down to his flat belly. I knew where I belonged.

Just getting my mouth open wide enough to get his plum-sized dickhead inside my mouth was a battle, though. Marines don't give up, so I finally made it and clamped my lips down hard, just behind his trigger-ridge. First, I slid my tongue around the impos-sibly soft skin of his cocksock, stripping away the sticky coating of pre-cum that he'd allowed to ooze out. He was sweet and thick, like corn syrup mixed with sweat. That leaky marine dick was the best thing I'd ever had inside my mouth — and I'd had a lot. I felt the ruffled 'skin that had lived in my dreams brush-ing against the back of my mouth, dripping its precious cargo onto the root of my tongue where I couldn't taste it. I clenched his 'skin tight and pulled my lips forward, working his cock out of my mouth until I was just locked onto his lizard by the snout, but now I was able to start stripping away his clear, jewel-like load of pre-cum. The tip of my tongue dipped for a moment into the pool crowning his cum-slit and pulled away. I felt a long string of his essence follow me away until it broke and tumbled to the bottom of my mouth. Unable to restrain my greed any longer, I let my mouthorgan slide into his cock-cowl, gliding between that tender 'skin and the impossibly firm and smooth pulsing meat that it kept safe and secret from the world. The taste of his pre-cum was sweet, but the farther back I slid, gliding across the smooth head and stripping away the day's scent along with the glorious goo he'd conjured just for me, the more other treasures I discovered. Don't get me worng; Keith keeps his dick clean. Still, he hadn't had a shower since morning, and a few carelessly shaken pisses, the sweat of a bootcamp day in the sun, and twenty hours of aging in the heat of his crotch had brewed so glorious a soup that I could have lived forever on nothing else. Like all uncut men, he was skittish about having me invade his secret landscape and shivered in delight when I slid my bumpy tongue across his treasure.

From the first taste of his dick, my mouth had been watering like a son-of-a-bitch, and now my spit flowed down into his cock-sock, filling the space and eating away at the sweat and musk that anchored his pre-cum. I slurped the brew out and chugged it down, but it only made me greedy for more. My tongue prodded deeper until I reached his trigger-ridge and the special treasures that he had kept hidden away there, even from his washcloth. My greed undid me, but it also undid him — filling his 'skin to the point where there wasn't room for both of us to frolic. His cock-cover unzipped back along his shaft like a convertible top in a car wash. When that flesh slid back and left his purple prick lying exposed and vulnerable to my lips, I slid those spit slicked cock-suckers across his manhood like Sherman through Georgia. His hips heaved up. The bastard even stopped pretending to be drunk. He yelled shit about how I was being too rough, that he wasn't used to having every nerve in his crank sucked apart, and shit along similar lines. I was too busy to answer, so I just sucked and lipped him harder. At one point, I even slid my teeth across his cockhead, not biting him, but I let him feel the sharp texture of my chompers and shiver with the thrill of what could be if he weren't very, very careful.

He kept bitching, louder and louder, but his dick knew what it craved: hot, tight flesh. Those strong hips humped up and rammed that huge manmeat deep into my throat, lodging it solid inside my tender tissues. I couldn't give him the tonguing I craved, but I could flex my throat and suck him like a starving lamprey. His hips found their rhythm and slid up, harder and faster and deeper into my throat until I felt his ballbag rise and knew I was seconds away from tasting the cream of the marines. I wasn't about to let him off so easy, though; I had worked too hard to get him there to satisfy myself with a twenty-minute suck. My face slid up his crank and let it fall against his hard, hairless belly with a wet THWACK that was still ricocheting off the walls when he started to go off on me for not being willing to suck his cock until he came in my mouth. By the time he'd realized how un-butch that would have sounded, I was up north, licking my way from his navel to his tits. My tongue slid around those hard knobs that crowned the best-developed chest I'd ever seen on a man until I'd fired them both up just fine. I let my lips glide up and down his tit-shafts, sucking lightly at first, then like a fiend as my lips picked up speed. In the end, flesh couldn't do the job and I had to gently grind his throbbing tits between my teeth until the bastard squirmed and screeched and moaned like no marine ever. I played those tits the way Rostropovitch plays the cello.

When I was finished stringing him along, rubbing him exactly the right way with every stroke, I moved up to lick my way across Keith's hairless pecs while my hands explored his flanks, glorying in his muscles and handling him like the stallion he was. His hips were grinding his crank into my belly all this time and I felt his ooze slime my gut, but somehow I didn't mind. He was obviously one of those lucky lads who had pre-cum the way Arabia has oil. I hadn't forgotten about that dick. After my adventures with his pecs and tits, though, I needed to lock lips with his. His bottom lip had reminded me of Ricky Nelson's — slightly pouty and down-turned, as though he never got what he really wanted. I sucked at that cute little lip and ran my tongue over and past it until I was inside his mouth sliding along his own mouth-muscle. His hands came into play, holding fast to the back of my head and grinding my face against his. I managed to escape for a moment to suck at his ear lobe. Don't ask me why, but I've always been an ear freak. There's just something meaty about the way it feels — and the way man reacts is epic. The dude has my hot, lust-driven breath jetting into his ear and is driven even further toward the brink. Sometimes, as that first night with Keith, I'll slide my wet tongue into his ear, flicking and fluttering about like a drunken butterfly until the poor bastard trapped below me is screaming for mercy. I never grant it, of course, but that's part of the pleasure, too.

Fucking with his ear, I could tell from the noise he was making and the rambunctious way his rod was rambling across my belly that it was time for me to suck some more dick. When I slid down, I left one hand up north to glide lightly across his washboard belly and firm, foxy flanks while I used the other to grab his balls and pull them tight, probe below into his ass-crack, and otherwise act like the lust-driven slut I was. Keith had cranked up a load of joint-juice while I'd been gone, so I started off by licking his belly clean and then re-stowed his massive marine meat back into my throat and turned up the suction. Incredibly, that cock had swollen even larger during its parole — and had picked up some bad habits, besides. Now his hips were more insistent, pushing and prodding deeper into my throat than ever before. I tried to keep up, but was just about to ease him out for a break to avoid passing out when I felt his cadence go to shit. His moans and grunts grew more feral: he was going to shoot. I felt his cum-tube pulse as that glorious jarhead jism rippled up from his balls and jetted down my throat. Too bad for me, he was so far down I couldn't taste shit. I held tight for about five more blasts and then pulled his head out into my mouth were my tongue could tear into him. His spooge was even sweeter than the pre-cum had been, but much more substantial. Thick threads of the frothy man-spunk dripped off the back of my mouth and down onto my tongue where every taste-bud came alive with protein-driven dreams of delight. I wasn't able to keep up with the blasts of his ball-juice, though, and had to chug his load down almost as fast as he blasted it into my waiting mouth. He shuddered and heaved and pounded and spurted for what seemed at the time like forever — or maybe an instant.

Time stood still for me then because I was in cocksucker heaven with that huge, hunky marine's joint spunking away in my mouth. On the other hand, looking back, I could have gone on forever chugging down his cum. The stingy bastard ran out much too soon — long before forever. I kept at it, though, until the final dribble and then slashed at his super-sensitive dick by way of punishment for leaving me dry. Uncut cock can't stand company after it's been used, so he gave me shit and finally pried my eager face off his joint. I moved back up to his mouth and eased the last three healthy salvos of jism into Keith's mouth so he could taste what he was made of. He was surprised for a moment, but then gave me a cum-eating grin that promised trouble to come. We made nice for a few minutes while he rested and, when I asked him what he wanted to get at next, he gave me a big, green-eyed, All-American smile and said the sweetest four words one man can use with another: "Would you fuck me?"

I've since discovered that most marines LOVE to have dick up their butts. I've never figured out why — maybe it's to show that they have what it takes. Maybe it's because they're proud of their asses. Personally, I can take dick up the ass or leave it alone. One as big as Keith's hurts so I have to really want to please when I spread my legs; I'm more a cocksucker. Later on, Keith showed that he could suck dick with the best of them, but *his* idea of a good time was to have my thick nine inches of marine muscle up his tight, jock ass. I'm essentially a nice guy. I'll give my buddies what they want. Before I tore him up, though, I was determined to go back down and scope out the cockpit between those righteous muscles. I rolled his ass over and used both hands to pry his tight cheeks apart. Pulsing pink and pretty at the bottom of his trench, this asshole looked like a dream come true. I slid my nose and mouth down, letting my tongue glide along that musky, hairless trench until I came to his fuckhole. Then I did a Mexican hat dance, darting around his pink folds and only now and again strafing across his hole in a cruel, gut-wrenching jolt that brought his ass up into my face from sheer reflex. My lips locked around that perfect pucker and my tongue started diving in, licking and lapping his musk, darting into his hole, and otherwise causing him all the delicious agony I could. The asshole moaned and bitched and begged for mercy knowing perfectly well that mercy was the one thing he'd never get from me.

When my tongue was about to fall out of my jaw and I knew I needed something to reach farther into his ass, I flipped him over, lifted his legs to the ceiling, and put my own best asset right where it belonged. I hung above him so I could see into those gorgeous green eyes at the moment we shared space. I needed to sear the image into my memory forever so when I was old, I could think back on that one perfect night and smile. Crinkles lurked in the corner of his eyes, as though his brain was afraid of what was coming; yet his soul knew he wanted my meat whatever the cost — because he craved personal contact with another human being after the brutalization of bootcamp, because he yearned to satisfy the ancient warrior's bond of physical intimacy, and, I like to think, because he wanted my studly marine body as much as I wanted his.

My thick dick slid inside his fuckhole almost as smoothly as my tongue had done before, but his face told me the difference. Those green eyes clenched shut as every muscle seized up at once to welcome me home where I belonged. I didn't insult him by asking if I should stop, but kept sliding down to glory. Clipping his prostate on the way by, I was rewarded by a shudder of such terrible delight that it started deep inside his guts and echoed through to every corner of his being. His jaw tried to relax to let a scream escape, but it was the most soul-felt of moans that slid up to envelope me in his pleasure. By the time I had parted the length of his tight, slick guts and nestled my swollen, throbbing dickhead deep in the welcome warmth of his jism-locker, Keith's green eyes were alive again, blazing satisfaction. I felt his shitchute grip my crankshaft even harder and playfully ripple against my flesh, pulling me downward with every undulation of his butt, claiming my meat as his. His hips arched up in craving, shafting ass even harder up my butt-buster, grinding his tortured hole against my stiff, rust-colored pubes as he groaned out like Dante's damned.

I stopped playing around and began fucking him like the slut he wanted to be. I tore into his butt, reaming and plunging deep until he writhed below me in delicious, exquisite agony. The way his body wrapped around my dick, the sight of his hunky body lying helpless below me, the ancient warrior bond we shared together, and, most of all, the rapine animal noises my fuck-thrusts tore from his soul all drove me on to even more feral frenzy. The sounds of our sweaty flesh crashing together flooded the room and washed civilization away. I was back in the primordial jungle where our kind began, fucking deep and hard by right of strength and conquest. Every vicious, careless plunge of my hard marine cock jabbed that jarhead ass closer to fulfilling his dreams and ass. I lost myself in my greedy, sordid pleasure until I wandered alone in the black void that lies deep within us all, where no man can look without knowing awe. I humped his hole forever, timelessly tearing into that tight manhole until eternity ended in a blinding flash of pain and light.

I came back to the world to hear screams of brutish lust rip from my snarling mouth and to feel my cock pulsing wide with load after creamy load of fresh, juicy, jarhead jism. Pounding everything I had up into that hungry butt, at last I found myself dry-humping my own leavings and collapsed atop him, one exhausted, sweaty, but very happy young marine. We lay together, catching our breath, until I felt the sweat begin to dry on my back. We had no time for rest, though. Keith and I were dedicated, young marines back then and knew the value of repeating a drill until we got it exactly right.

FOXY MARINE

RICK JACKSON, USN

I NOTICED THE FOXY MARINE the moment I boarded the tail car of the San Diego Trolley. He stood out something fierce. It was 11:50 of a Thursday night, and downtown San Diego was almost deserted. Even if Brent had been hidden in the background of a fuck-flick, though, his body and smile were fine enough that my lizard would have done somersaults. Alone on the car, he was all I could see. I don't need to spell out how a young lance corporal's pecs, crowned with hard, meaty tits, fill out his t-shirt or how flat and tight and savory his gut is. Unless you've spent your life in a cave, you know all about marine muscle.

Brent was more than just a well-built animal set for stud. He was cute as a bug's ear besides. At 19, standing 5'9" with blond hair and the greenest eyes outside the cat family, he wore a boyish grin set in a warrior's jaw, blending youth and a studly sensuality hot enough to melt molybdenum. I sat helpless, gawking at his reflection in the windows as we slid along through the night. Once or twice, I thought I saw him aim a sly, sidelong glance at me, but I wasn't sure until we'd passed Market. When no one got on at the transfer station, I took the chance and walked over to his seat. Tough as they come, I sneered down into his Luke-Skywalker face and said, "If you want to suck it, marine, just say so."

His foxy face flashed through a dozen emotions from fear to shock to delight. Then he grinned like a fool and said, "So."

I tore off my t-shirt and ripped open the buttons on my trou. My butt-starved lizard slammed up against my bare belly with a no-nonsense SMACK that echoed up and down the car. Like any highly trained marine fighting machine, once the beach was clear, young Brent didn't waste any time charging my rampart. He sucked my swollen, pre-cum oozing dickhead into his cute little face in one swift, relentless motion. When my meat was warm and slathered in spit, he eased it out again so he could lap up my shaft like any other spaniel with a meaty bone. Now and again, he'd give me a break and let my dick slide back into his mouth for a moment's tongue-lashing. The slut couldn't get enough of my sweet pre-cum. Once I was licked clean, his rough tongue would start to spin around my swollen meathead like a buzz-saw in a tornado until every nerve ending was aching for a time out.

He was interested in more than my meat, though: his tongue loved to lap at my ballbag, knocking my nuts around with his prodding nose and jarhead mouthorgan. He sank his face deep into my crotch to breathe in great lungfuls of my nasty, smelly man-musk while he worked. His lips took time out to kiss and suck at my thighs with the same fervor a Hari Krishna goes af-ter airport donations. His lips and tongue pummeled my balls. Often as not, they ended up being sucked into his mouth so he could gnaw lightly at my spooge-lockers as he sucked on them like some protein-hungry vampire. But as I leaned up against the seat opposite his, my feet spread wide in the aisle so he could work his marine magic, most of his sucking was concentrated on the thick nine inches of raw need that pulsed and throbbed be-tween us. Whenever my dick would begin to dry out, his tongue slipped up from my wet balls and spread satisfaction in his path. That bumpy, serpentine tongue slathered spit across my shaft, slamming here and there as every heartbeat pumped even more passion into my butt-buster, until his young face and my hard, naked belly were both dripping wet.

While his tongue was driving every frazzled nerve in my joint frantic, the slut man-handled my ass, too. His strong hands ripped my butt cheeks wide so his finger could slither down my dank, nasty ass-crack. I knew what he was looking for, but he seemed in no hurry to find it. He prodded and stroked and slid those magic fingers of his as though we had years instead of only a few miles to do The Deed. At any stop, some geek could climb aboard the car and find us. I should have been worried, but his face and body were so choice, I was willing to risk almost any-thing. When his fingers finally found my fuckhole, he didn't pry it open as a sailor would have. He rubbed and tickled and pinched my tight squid butthole, knowing from experience how fine he could make me feel. Like most marines, he was a bottom at heart and didn't need his dick up my butt. What he needed most in the world just then was my best asset up his tight, marine hole.

I felt my hips swaying back and forth as his fingers went seriously to work, massaging my fuckhole with a delicious, regular, hypnotic motion unlike anything I'd ever known. As his fingers dried out, he'd scoop a swath of spit off my balls so the gentle, relentless circles he was tracing across my asshole would lull me even deeper into the limp limbo of lust. I remember giving up his face long enough to pull off his shirt so I could run my hands across his broad, muscle-knotted shoulders as well as through that short-cropped jarhead haircut. The combination of Brent's fingers playing at my ass and his tongue twisting around my joint seduced me into a stupor that grew richer and more mesmerizing with every delicious stroke. The leathernecked cockhound would probably still be grinding away at my crotch if he hadn't eased his face one time too many over the swollen knob slipping and sliding against my belly. When his lips slithered their way across my purple throb, something inside my guts snapped. I felt my balls explode and the load of my young life shoot up through my tortured dick. As the frothy cream surged north, my cum-tube streched until I thought the head of my dick was ready to pop off. I heaved and rammed and pounded my meat into that cute marine face, grinding his pug nose into my stiff, rust-colored pubes, and heard him gurgle and sputter like a clogged up drain. Brent knew the taste of quality cream. His lips and throat sucked away the haze of ecstasy bred by his butt massage. One second I was lost in a daze; the next, my hands wrapped around the back of his neck and my squid dick was reaming so far down his tight marine throat that I polished his tonsils. One spasm after another shook me rigid. All I could do was try to hold onto the vulpine head bobbing off the end of my cock as my guts turned inside out and shot creamy fire down Brent's spunk-sucking throat. I half heard my grunts and moans of satisfaction ricocheting inside the car. The lights streaking past outside were as unreal as the perfection of that throat or the hands clawing at my ass or the feel of my load being sucked up out of my balls like some long, very prickly worm. I must have blacked out for a time. When I came back to life, my hands were pulling at his ears like bootstraps, and I was dry-humping his facehole. I remember giving Brent's jarhead a few good last thrusts to show him who was boss, and then pried him off my nine hard inches of nautical weapon.

He tenderly kissed my thighs and thanked me. I think the goof was trying to work his way back to rim my hole when I pulled him to his feet. While I was busy having my way with him, he had worked his dick out of his jeans. I grabbed a handful and twisted his foreskin back along the shaft so I could see what he had. He had plenty: a plum-sized purple dickhead that had my name all but engraved on it. I slid my fist forward and tore off a twisting handful of his man-scent. He kept his gear clean, but I could smell the unmistakable musk of a man: stale sweat blended with perhaps a hint of some carelessly shaken piss and aged to perfection inside his soft cocksock. I knew that before I let him escape, I'd have that dick down my own throat, savoring its taste and smell as much as I savored the sight of his studly young body. First, though, I knew what he needed more than anything: the fuck of his young life.

Knowing marines, I saw he wanted to spread right then; but I wanted to taste my cum on his lips. I wanted to suck lightly on his ear lobe and maybe drill my tongue inside. I wanted to lose myself in the crystal depths of his green eyes and hold his hard, lean body in my arms. I reached down and cupped his classic butt, lifting him slightly and pulling him hard against my naked, heaving flesh as we jostled through the night, rattling together in the Trolley's rhythm until our stiff manhoods tangled between our bellies, fighting like elk at the rut. I kissed his neck and slid my nails up and down his spine until I heard a moan escape from the depths of his soul that said everything. It said, "Please . . . Fuck me — hard — NOW." It begged for my strength and my tenderness, for my mastery and my love — at least for a moment. After surviving boot camp and the brutal, faceless life of the Corps for so long, he needed to connect with another human being — to have part of someone else deep inside him. My lips coasted down to his shoulders, and I felt his tits grow even harder with yearning as they drilled through the thick red thatch covering my chest as our bodies lurched and scraped together. Suddenly he moaned again, a soft, almost subsonic "Pleeaaaass-sssseeee." I let my hands slide from his butt for a moment as he was already turned around, draped over the back of a seat.

Any other time, I'd have made it my business to stop and admire what he had. The Corps really does build men — and especially butts. Most marines have fine, hard butts that jut straight out at you and seem to hang magically suspended, just waiting for your meat to slide between them. Brent's had the extra bonus of being soft-skinned and hairless. As I slid my butt-buster between those massive mounds of marine man-muscle, I felt his super-soft skin stretched over clumps hard as carbon steel. When my dick skated down that smooth, hairless trench, I realized the hole I was about to claim would be even better than Brent's face. I reached around to grab his tits, pulling them slightly to confuse the pain of my crashing through into his shit-chute. I began gently prodding against his hole and felt his pink muscles nibble at my lizard's snout, inviting me in. My hips began to arc up a little harder with every stroke, pounding now against his fuckhole so that eventually I'd break through into glory. Brent wasn't about to wait for eventually, though. He was a desperate young man in one very quick hurry. He wasn't interested in gentle, civilized love-making; he wanted me to fuck him up the butt. His asshole flew back in one swift, cruel lunge that would have sent me reeling if his hole hadn't already eaten my meat for breakfast. I felt that starving, slick marine shit-chute slam up over my throbbing dickhead, streak across my trigger-ridge, glide up my crankshaft, and wrap itself tightly into my pubes. I cupped his pecs in my hands and felt his hard tits drilling into my palms. Looking down over his shoulders, I saw his hands gripping the seat back with white knuckles, but the way his head was thrown back and the open-mouthed moans of pleasure ripped from his soul told a different story. If his body was having a hard time, his spirit was soaring.

Brent's hot marine butt cinched itself around my crankshaft like the final voice of doom. He eased himself down my thick shaft, milking me for every sensation he could find. Then, once he'd found my trigger-ridge again with the tight sphincters holding me prisoner, he arched his ass up a little, flared his fuckhole for a moment, and used a Marlene Dietrich tone in his studly masculine voice to say, ''Go to it, squid-dick. Show me what you can do.''

If he wanted it rough, that was fine with me. I shoved his head down, grabbed his hips, and started slamming my butt-buster harder and faster up into his hungry hole with every stroke. The SMACK of flesh against hard, sweaty flesh counted my cadence; his feral groans and moans of ecstasy urged me onward. Every stroke of my man-meat up his slutty marine fuckhole was different. Sometimes he'd grip my lizard hard enough to strangle it; other times he would let his muscles ripple up and down my shaft like a flute solo. When I found his prostate and crashed into it whenever I could, I felt him give an extra-special squeal of delight. Sometimes shivers or goose bumps would roll across his hard, naked flesh and his hole would grind itself into my wiry pubes on the in-stroke. Sometimes I just held him tight for a moment and let the thwackety-thwack of the train vibrate his shit-chute along my thick dick. I wrapped one arm under his belly to claim absolute control of the action — and to free my other arm to grab his nuts now and again or tweak his tits or coast up along his strong flanks while I fucked the living shit out of his ass. Each time my cum-slit slammed into the end of his fuck-tunnel, he'd grunt in satisfaction. When I hunched over him like a cur dog with a mongrel bitch and skimmed my lips across his neck, he purred like the slut he was. I licked the sweat from his neck and ear while I reamed his hole, heaving him harder and faster against the seat while the city slid past. My hips were on auto-pilot now, fucking for their own pleasure rather than his. I wasn't making love; I was reaming ass. I wasn't a noble defender of freedom — or even a sailor on liberty; I was a jungle animal turned loose on a piece of fresh meat. My dick ate nine inches of his butt with every vicious bite, and always had room to tear off another piece. I felt his ass respond to my abuse, rising relentlessly to skewer his virtue on the lance of my lust. Time seemed to slide along on rails as smooth and relentless as the Trolley. My fucking dick began to glow and then to burn from friction, but I knew Brent was warming his ass on our fire so I just turned up the heat. Soon, hunched over his lean, killing-machine body, I lost control even of memory and lost myself in the timeless mist of instincts older than man himself.

I heard three voices. I recognized Brent's "Ohhh! Jeess-sssuuusssss, Yeeeessssss!" first. Then I heard mine, grunting and slavering like the depraved rapine beast he had made me as I had made him. The third voice took longer. Then I realized it was the Trolley announcer over the 1-MC say that we'd reached the border. We'd overshot 32nd Street and had all but left the country. I opened my eyes at last to discover Brent was bent, ass-up, over the back of a seat — and I was still on top of him, sunk to the hilt in the juiciest, most spooge-filled butt of modern times. My teeth were locked into his strong shoulder, forcing his head onto the seat. My butt was aimed at the ceiling — not exactly the way I wanted to be caught. I lifted us off the seat and was disappointed to see Brent had blasted his load all over his belly and the plastic seat. I'd had other plans for his creamy jism.

I knew the Trolley driver would be coming down to our end of the train any second to start the last run back up to San Diego. Time was the one thing we didn't have. I unplugged the best hole I'd found in a very long time and ordered Brent to pull his act together. I couldn't resist reaching down to the seat to scoop up a handful of his Grade-A, USMC Prime to taste what he had. Then I realized what being at the border really meant and changed my mind. I made him lick his spooge from my hand as we, somehow, pulled our clothes on and were out the door before the driver showed up.

I saw my little fuck-toy was still confused, so I spelled it out for him: we'd overshot the base. We didn't have to be back on base until 0700. We were yards from Tijuana — where there were more sleazy, no-questions-asked cheap hotel rooms than anywhere else on the planet. Now did he want to grab a room and let me lick the marine cream off his chest before I fucked him again and made him fuck me until we were both rubbed raw — or did he want to climb back onto the Trolley and go home.

No one ever said marines are quick, bless them; but I saw his face change as he squinted at the Trolley and then looked at me and the border crossing. That grin came back and widened to shit-eating proportions until he patted my ass and said, "Home? No, somehow I think we *are* home." They may not be quick, but marines do catch on. Besides, they ARE very nice to have around.

FLYBOY

WILLIAM COZAD

I WAS A JUNIOR IN college when I decided that I wanted to check out the gay lifestyle. I mean, I'd tried it with a chick and it was a disaster. If that's all there is, like Peggy Lee sings, then break out the booze. Along about this time there were raids by the campus pigs on the library toilet for alleged homosexual activity. Word was that the action moved to the toilet in the commons.

By now I had a real case of blue balls from thinking about it, and I went to that toilet to see if I could find some relief. There was cocksucking going on all right; it took place between the stalls. When I figured out what to do, I poked my dick through the hole in the partition and into a hot, wet mouth. I worked up such a wad that the cocksucker practically choked. He spit it out anyway. I don't know why.

That satisfied and it didn't. Something was missing, like knowing the other person. I was kind of shy and just couldn't hit on my buddies. They all liked girls. I didn't want to ruin my reputation. Say what you will, in those days they might've called you an artist in France but here they called you a cocksucker.

I liked to take breaks from my studying. I'd go downtown and look at the stuff in the stores. I'd look at men too. There's something really sexy about a sweaty man who works with his hands, I find, even if he goes home to fuck his wife and argue about money and watch television. Boring. I could never live that way.

Stopping in a restaurant, I ordered a cup of coffee at the counter. I needed to wake up and get back to my studies. Sitting at the counter was a guy about my age wearing a blue Air Force uniform. I'd seen R.O.T.C. cadets on campus in military uniform but hadn't paid much attention to them. Here was the real thing, a young soldier. Not only that but he was a hunk, cute and macho, like the young men you see in the recruiting posters.

Oh, I think I'm falling in love, I told myself. He had sort of a shaggy flattop. And blue eyes, as blue as the wild blue yonder. I lit up a cigarette. I was trying to quit smoking but the filthy habit relaxed me. I started smoking in high school after I saw all those cute boys do it in that movie, "The Outsiders." There was Matt Dillon, C. Thomas Howel, Ralph Macchio and Rob Lowe. That's when I started to take a closer look around the locker room at school, too.

The waitress was jawing with the cook. There was no cream for my coffee. I asked the airman to pass the cream, please. He did and gave me a smile that took my breath away. He had the most sensuous lips, kind of pouty and ruby red. I kept staring at him.

"Where are you stationed?"

"Mt. Tam."

"Mt. Tamalpais?"

"Yeah, there's an Air Force radar station on top of it."

"Really?"

That surprised me. Of course I didn't know much about the military, except that our government spent most of the budget on defense. R.O.T.C. cadets weren't popular, not like jocks, on campus.

I sipped my coffee and puffed my cigarette, hoping I didn't look as nervous as Don Knotts. I didn't know what else to say to him. You can't say what you think, like you're beautiful, I want to marry you, at least kiss your cock. The waitress refilled our coffee cups. And the airman moved next to me to use the cream pitcher.

"You live around here?" he asked.

"Yeah. I go to college."

"I wasn't much good in school. That's why I joined the Air Force. Well, not exactly."

"Huh?"

"A buddy and I went joyriding. The judge said go to the military or jail. Beats being locked up. Besides, I'd always heard the Air Force was best, you know their survival kit is an all-electric kitchen."

I smiled. He extended his hand and said his name was Brian. The nameplate on his uniform said Morgan.

"Bill is the alias under which I'm currently circulating."

He smiled back.

"What do you do for fun around here?"

"I go to movies."

"You wanna go to the movies?"

"I've got to study."

What the hell was I saying? Got to study indeed. I'd lived for twenty years and not seen a man as good-looking as Brian Morgan. I'd go to a movie. Hell, I'd go anywhere with him.

"That's too bad. I'm just a lonely soldier. Even my roommate is on leave."

"Don't you live in a barracks?"

"Nope. The Air Force has, like, dorms."

I sipped the last of my coffee. It tasted bitter. Like life, I thought, if I let Brian get away from me.

"Let's go to the movies," I said.

"What's playing?"

"I dunno. You like surprises?"

"Sure."

While I fumbled for change in my pocket, Brian paid the tab. I left the waitress a tip.

The Bijou on Main Street played old movies. "Hud" was showing, starring Paul Newman.

Brian bought the tickets, saying he's just gotten paid. I bought a tub of popcorn that would've been big enough for all the airmen on the mountaintop to snack on. And I'd sure like to snack on them, at least on Brian.

He commented on what a heel womanizing Hud Bannon was. I thought about how good-looking Paul Newman was in his beefcake days. Through the movie we munched on popcorn and lived through the cattle epidemic which destroyed the ranch and granddad. The slatternly housekeeper moved on. Lonnie the nephew struck out on his own. Hud stayed on to let them drill for oil on the land where the cattle had roamed.

After the movie, Brian and I went outside. It was night and chilly.

"I'd better hit the books," I said.

I knew the airman's name, where he was stationed. I could send him a letter and invite him to go somewhere, maybe a play on campus, a football game, although nobody remembered the last time our team won.

"Want to go back to the base with me? See my mountaintop home?"

137

"I'd like to go but it's getting late."

"You can stay the night."

That idea made my toes curl. Not to mention the fire spreading in my loins. He couldn't be thinking the same thing I was. He was a healthy, red-blooded American boy. He had to be horny. No, he was just lonely and wanted company. But he could hang out with his buddies on the base.

I don't know how he maneuvered it all but I went along with him. His bedroom eyes promised a good time. We took the bus to the base, a climb up to the top of Mt. Tamalpais. It was night and foggy and I couldn't see much.

I accompanied Brian onto the base, and then to his room. There were two small beds, a desk and chair.

He stripped and carefully hung up his uniform. His body was solid and hairy, contrasting my smooth body. He slept in GI white cotton boxer shorts. I shucked my duds down to my Jockey shorts, trying to hide my semi-hard cock.

Brian doused the light. I crawled into the other airman's bunk. Silver moonlight penetrated the fog and spilled into the room.

Just being in the room alone with the butch, handsome airman made me horny. My cock was throbbing. I listened to his even breathing. I wanted to beat off. Instead I tossed and turned.

"Come over here," he said. "Sleep with me."

He held up the covers and I slipped into his bed. It was dangerous, fooling around on a military base. Homosexuality was taboo. If I had doubts about Brian before, I didn't now. He was just lonely, horny, wanted to jack-off probably.

Wrapped in his arms, I felt his hairy chest and smelled his musky body. He was sweaty and breathing heavy. His hairy legs pressed against mine and I could feel his fiery, hard prick. My cock tented my shorts and leaked pre-cum. I reached between his legs and grabbed his cock inside his boxers, and he groped me.

"Oh Brian, you're so damn beautiful."

"Suck me. I want you to suck my dick."

I wanted romance and he wanted sex. He'd think of me as just a cocksucker. He was taking a big chance, the way the military felt about queers, by taking me on the base with him.

Throwing off the covers, my eyes feasted on his strong, hairy body in the puddle of silvery moonlight. I tugged down his boxers and he kicked them off. I peeled off my Jockeys. Holding his veiny shaft with the crimson mushroom head, I noted the strand of pre-cum.

"Lick it," he moaned.

I swabbed my tongue over his spongy cockhead and tasted the saline goo.

"Put it in your mouth, man."

I yawned and stretched my lips around the young airman's bulbous cockhead. I held onto the throbbing shaft while I swirled my tongue over his cockhead and licked the ridge below the crown. I jacked on the shaft while I sucked his cockhead.

"You like that, don't you? You like sucking my big cock."

"Mmm," I replied, not missing a beat, rotating my mouth on his cockhead while I stroked the shaft.

"Eat it, man. Take it all down you throat. Yeah, that's it. Feels good. Suck that motherfucker."

By now I had my other hand wrapped around my own dick and was beating it in synch with sucking the airman's cock.

He pulled his cock out of my mouth.

"Lick my balls. Oh yeah. Chew on those suckers."

I did what Brian asked. No one had ever talked to me before during sex, just slurping, moaning and groaning sounds. Brian showed that he could give orders as well as take them.

His balls were big and hairy and loaded with cum, I could tell. His cock was like a missile in a silo waiting to explode. I swallowed those orbs one at a time, got both of them into my mouth and hummed on them.

"Stop, man. I'm so fucking hot. I don't wanna cum yet."

To take his mind off his impending orgasm, I guess, Brian reached down between my legs and grabbed my cock. His strong, hot hand jacked my dick. He surprised me when he turned around into a sixty-nine position. I figured him for what they called trade. You could suck his dick but he wouldn't reciprocate. Boy, was I wrong. Brian gobbled up my dick and sucked like a champ. All the while he tugged on my nuts, driving me crazy, almost to the point of orgasm before he stopped.

After he showed me that he wasn't afraid of 69, that no cock scared him, he didn't reach for the mouthwash, but climbed on top of me and sat on my face.

"Eat that ass."

I hesitated. I'd fooled around at the glory hole, letting guys kiss my cock and kissing some of them but I'd never kissed any fart boxes.

"Stick that tongue up my ass, man. Yeah, that's it. Poke it in and out. Oh yeah, eat that butthole."

His asshole was hairy but like they say, once you get past the smell you've got it licked. It didn't smell bad at all, kind of soapy from his shower that day, kind of sweaty. Tangy. Yeah, that's it.

Brian sat on my face. He reached back and pulled my prick while I rimmed him.

"Oh, that gets me hot. So fucking hot."

He held my cock while he speared his ass on it. I couldn't believe it! Not this macho airman! But he did. I'd never gone in the back door before. It was so hot and tight, that butthole, lubed with spit, and I could feel the hairs in his asshole tickle my shaft. Like a rubber ball, he bounced his ass around on my cock. It was the hottest, most pleasurable sensation I'd ever felt.

"Fuck me," he growled. "Fuck that ass."

I held onto his asscheeks while I thrust upwards into his butthole. Oh God, I wondered, what would happen if somebody heard us, what if they caught us? That made it all the more dangerous and exciting.

The cum was boiling in my balls. It rushed up my tube and exploded into the airman's ass, wads of hot, juicy jism. He clamped his ass muscles around my cock and milked it. He reached back and squeezed my balls. It was by far the most powerful orgasm, the biggest load I'd ever shot. And it squirted deep into the airman's chute. His cock gyrated from the shattering load that shot up his ass.

He collapsed on top of me. My cock plopped out of his fuckhole. He was breathing heavy. I could feel his cock poke against my belly. I could feel cum drip out of his ass and down onto my own thighs.

Brian sat up on my crotch. He pinched my tits and tugged on my nipples. No one had ever done that to me before. I felt a big rush, like a jolt of electricity shot through my body. He got between my legs and lifted them in the air. I wanted to protest that I couldn't do it, I couldn't take a cock up the ass, not a massive fucker like his. Instead I scissored my legs around his hips. He just spit down on his cock and rubbed it over the head. Positioning his boner at the entrance to my cherry butthole, he sank his cockhead inside.

His cock hurt like hell. But I wanted it, despite the pain. I wanted the airman's cock inside me. He inched the shaft up my hole and waited a moment.

"Oh fuck. It hurts but I don't care. Do it. Fuck my ass. Fuck me, Brian. Hurt me. I want it. Awww, keep fucking me."

The pain subsided and my ass was crammed with cock for the first time. I wanted it, every inch of that big cock inside me. I started moving my ass around and fucking back at that monstrous cock.

Brian sweat like a hog while he pumped my asshole, reaming me good. I could take it, whatever he gave, because I wanted it so bad. His sweat dripped onto my body. He sat back on his heels and watched his big cock disappear up my ass.

My head jerked from side to side. I pulled him back down on top of me. His lips crushed against mine. I opened my mouth and accepted his probing tongue, which licked my teeth. I sucked on his tongue while he banged my ass. His big, hairy, cum-laden nuts slapped against my asscheeks while he relentlessly pistoned my hole. Connected tongue to mouth, cock to ass, he rammed me.

He came up for air. Gasping and groaning, drenched in sweat, he lunged his steely-hard cock inside to the hilt and my ass exploded like it was a keg of dynamite and his cock was a blowtorch.

The earth shook, the mountain tumbled to the ocean. Rivulets of molten cum, like fire from a volcano, spewed into my bowels. My asshole clamped around that exploding cock and I held onto Brian for dear life, clawing his back and clutching his furry asscheeks, making sure that I got every inch of cock, every drop of his cum inside me.

Both of us were panting hard when his cock softened and slithered out of my satiated hole. He'd quenched the fires of lust inside me with his precious cum and I knew that I'd never be the same again, that I'd always want cock, that I'd always want Brian.

He held me in his arms and stroked my hair. In the afterglow I could feel the connection, the union completed. I felt more alive than I'd ever felt before.

I touched the swirls of hair on his chest. I pressed my cheek against his.

"Kiss me, you fool," I said.

He laughed, then kissed me tenderly.

"Get in the other bed, man. We can't let them catch us asleep in each other's arms."

"Yeah, you're right."

I located my Jockeys on the floor. Brian's boxers were tangled up in the sheets. I kissed him one more time and crawled into the other bunk and went out like a light.

At dawn I awoke to all the strange noises and voices outside the room.

Brian was getting dressed in his work clothes. He smiled at me and I melted. If I thought the night before was just a wild, wet dream, my sore butt let me know otherwise.

For a moment I felt panicky, like I wasn't supposed to be there on the base. Like they'd catch me and call the civilian cops. Maybe I'd go to jail for trespassing, whatever.

I worried for nothing. Brian took me to the mess hall for breakfast. Actually it was more like a dining room with small tables. The food was good, a helluva lot better than the garbage they served on campus that you had to pay for. He even introduced me as his cousin to some of his buddies.

Brian had to go to work but I made sure he had my phone number. He promised to call the next weekend. He did. I was obsessed with him. It was like I couldn't live without him. A note, a phone call, made my head spin.

I lived in a rooming house off campus. The old lady was strict about visitors, no partying. When I introduced my — uh — cousin Brian, she took an instant liking to him. She'd lost a son in Vietnam. In fact, she even let him into my room when I wasn't there. Let me tell you what a joy it is to come home and find a naked airman sleeping in your bed. They say that flyboys cum in the air. Well, not mine. Not my Brian.

SAILOR'S SURPRISE

WILLIAM COZAD

A FTER NAVY BOOT CAMP I went home on leave. I was proud of my uniform and that I finally belonged somewhere. I felt like I had a real future ahead of me.

The old hometown was pretty quiet, with not much happening. I worked a bit on my car; my mom drove it now. Since I had time and was kind of bored, I mowed the lawn and painted some rooms in the house to earn my keep.

At night I ended up driving around downtown, drinking a lot of coffee and sodas at the fast food places. I saw some of the gang from high school but most had gone away to college or just moved on.

I even left town a couple days early. In my imagination I thought things would be the same. Only *I* would be different because I was a sailor now. But I was just as lonely as I was when I left to join up, if not more so. The town looked the same, but the people seemed to have changed.

I rode the bus to San Francisco to pick up my ship, the U.S.S. *Interdiction*, a radar picket ship in the Seventh Fleet, the Pacific.

I had hoped I was going to have a wild time on leave like a lot of the guys in boot camp talked about — going home and getting laid. I was sure disappointed. About the only time people had noticed me was when I went to church with Mom and wore my uniform.

The only sexy thing that had happened recently occurred in boot camp. There was one sailor there that I really admired. Idolized would be closer to the truth. He was a short guy named Frank from Texas. I think he was a half-breed of some kind, judging by his exotic features, the ruddy complexion and high cheekbones. But what really made him different was the huge cock and balls that swung between his legs. I'd checked him out in the showers, and he was living proof that things were bigger in the Lone Star state.

He was friendly too. He'd done construction work and had a powerful, muscular body. Calisthenics were a piece of cake for him, while most of us huffed and puffed, strained and sweated. Our company commander got us all into shape pretty fast. And I actually felt a lot better with a leaner, harder body, though I sure missed a lot of sleep in basic training.

One night when I went to the head to take a leak I saw Frank there. He seemed out of breath, quickly washing his hands and leaving.

"How's it going, mate?"

"Better after taking a big shit."

I smiled back at him. I took a leak, then it dawned on me that maybe Frank had been beating his meat, maybe that was why he was all flushed and winded. I decided to take a look in the end stall where he'd been.

On the black toilet seat there was a drop of liquid. *Cum?* Maybe it was just a piss drop. I rubbed it with my finger, it was sticky and had that metallic smell of jizz. My cock boinged into a super boner.

Crazy and horny for Frank, I just smeared that cum on my cock and started jerking it. Seated on the commode where Frank's warm ass had been just moments ago, I hurriedly whipped off a load. I didn't even care that the guy on guard duty might catch me and report me. There was a rumor that a sailor who'd been kicked out for being "Unsuitable for military service" had actually been caught masturbating. They said that was the real reason for his discharge.

The reason for *my* discharge was Frank. How I idolized him. He might have been just some Texas hick, but to me he was the ideal man. If I had doubts about my attraction to guys, Frank made me realize the truth. Even though to him I was probably just another boot buddy. That night I had a dream about him and woke up with my hard cock twitching and shooting off. Yeah, I thought, it's *men* that I want.

In San Francisco I got a room at the Armed Forces YMCA on the waterfront, rather than staying at Treasure Island until my ship arrived. I drank a lot of beer at a sleazy bar and got tanked, then passed out drunk in my room.

The next day — after drinking a lot of coffee — I felt better. I rode a cable car, then walked around Chinatown and Fisherman's Wharf.

I had just one more night before my ship arrived and I had to report aboard. I ate a big meal in the restaurant downstairs and decided to hit the hay. But I was restless with anticipation, and horny. I couldn't sleep. I kept thinking about Frank, about that drop of his cum I found on the toilet seat; I remembered wiping his cream on my dick and beating off.

I decided to take a shower. It was late and I didn't expect anyone to be in the shower room.

There was a guy standing at the pisser with his dick out. Looked a bit stiff to me. Another guy was seated on a toilet in the stall behind him.

Water was running in the showers. I had just a towel around my waist and my room key in my hand. There was a lot of steam in the shower area. I took a spot under one of the nozzles and adjusted the water. There was another guy showering but I couldn't see him clearly.

I soaped up and rinsed off, the water cascading down my body, relaxing me. I washed my cock and balls, lathered them up. My cock wanted more attention but I restrained myself.

The haze in the shower began to lift and I saw this big blond dude. He was like a god. Sparkling blue eyes. Smooth, muscular body. Big uncut cock, with heavy low-hangers. He looked to be in his early twenties.

"Feels good, the shower," I said.

I was kind of nervous around him.

"Sure does."

I thought he'd leave but he stayed there under the spray of water. He had the perfect body; chiseled features, great shape, and that big dick.

"Busy night," I said.

I didn't really know what I meant by that, except that there were other people in the toilet.

"Yeah. Uh, soap my back, I'll soap yours."

"Okay."

I quickly realized that wasn't just idle conversation — I saw his cock lengthen a bit, the head peeking out of its thick hood. Myself, I sprang a boner right away. I tried to turn toward the wall, but I know he saw it.

He turned the other showers on — hot — and steam filled the

room again. He soaped my back first. I tingled all over from his touch.

He handed me the soap and I lathered his back. My mind was racing. Maybe he did just want a helping hand — but why had he turned on all the hot water? So no one could see us?

He turned back around and his cock brushed my thigh. It was hard, no doubt about it. With the soap in my hand I circled my strokes lower and lower till I was sudsing his cock and balls. His meat grew into a huge hard-on.

Maybe I'd got myself into something I couldn't handle. I was hotter than hell and ready to pop my nuts. When the blond stud took the soap and lathered up my genitals I don't know how I kept from shooting my load. He rubbed my buttcheeks and the cleft. Nobody had ever touched me there before. His finger probed at my butthole.

With the water spraying down on me, I watched the blond sink to his knees. He held my stiff cock out and licked it. His tongue was like fire. He fastened his lips around my burning dickhead. God, I'd never felt anything so incredible before. It definitely made jacking off seem like kid's stuff.

I caressed his wet blond locks and pumped my prick into his throat. He clasped my buttcheeks, then held onto my thighs as I bucked.

"Oh shit! Fuck! I'm gonna fucking shoot!"

He didn't back off a bit and suddenly I just gushed, shot my hot cum down the blond guy's throat. He took it all, swallowing and grunting. I heard him licking and smacking his lips as he eased my dickhead out of his mouth.

Getting to his feet, he sort of spun me around, away from the shower spray and pushed me down to my knees. In the gray haze of the shower I faced my first hard cock. I was a little scared. Could I go through with it? Maybe I should tell him I wasn't queer, that I didn't suck cock.

But I *wanted* to taste his cock, to lick that big bouncing dick, put it in my mouth and suck on it, feel it swell and shoot, drink his hot cum like he did mine.

I didn't have time to mull the idea over — that throbbing pecker was pushed right between my lips. I held the broad base to keep from being choked to death. With that pulsing prick in my grasp

I chewed on the foreskin and worked my tongue inside to lick the flared cockhead.

"Suck my balls, boy."

I held that manmeat and jacked it while I obeyed him. I licked his nuts and sucked them into my mouth. His equipment tasted all soapy and spongy but I didn't care.

"Get back on that dick."

He gave a lot of orders, but since boot camp I was used to being told what to do. I stretched my lips around that fucker and sucked on it.

At that moment all my doubts were gone. I knew for sure that I was queer, a cocksucker, whatever. And I didn't fight it. Let the Navy catch me, put me in the brig, I didn't care. I'd waited all my life for this, for real sex with a man.

I nursed on that cock while I rubbed his wet blond bush. I fondled those big cum-laden balls. I clutched his rock-hard buns while I sucked the daylights out of him.

And he enjoyed it, if his moans and groans were any indication.

"Oh fuck, I'm cumming. Take it, guy. Eat my fuckin' wad!"

His hot fuckjuice sprayed my tonsils. Novice cocksucker that I was, I couldn't swallow it all, no matter how hard I tried. His cock lurched out of my mouth and spit cum drops all over my face.

I licked up what I could and rinsed off under the shower.

"Let's go to my room."

"Sure," I agreed quickly.

His room was like mine, a closet-sized space with a narrow bed, but on the top floor of the building. There was light from outside, making shadows, and you could hear the roar of traffic from down on the freeway ramp.

The blond had a bottle of whiskey and we both drank from it.

"Jim Beam," I noted.

"That's me."

I laughed at his joke. I wasn't much of a drinker, except for beer. But the whiskey gave me a buzz and made me glow inside.

"What kind of work do you do?"

"Electronics, radar. Government gig. You?"

"I'm a sailor."

He gave me a real startled look.

"Oh?"

He took another big swig. I didn't think much more about it. The military wasn't popular since the Vietnam war. But it was my ticket out of my dull hometown and the chance for a college education later on.

"Relax," I said. "I don't bite. That was my first time — but I guess you could tell."

"No, not really. You're a very good looking kid."

"So are you. Matter of fact, you're about the best looking dude I've ever seen."

"Have another drink," he offered.

"Don't mind if I do."

He relaxed, slipped the towel off his waist and then removed mine. He pulled me down on top of him. Our hands roamed over each other's body. Our cocks rubbed against each other.

"Know what I really want?"

"Anything you like," I replied.

I was higher than a kite. And then he kissed me. It was like an explosion. I saw stars. Tasted whiskey. Kissing my girl after the senior prom had been nothing like this.

The blond grabbed my stiff prick and squeezed.

"Beautiful dick. Big mushroom head. Nice curve. Veiny and meaty. Hard as a carp."

No one had ever noticed my dick before. At least they'd never said anything about it. Girls had liked me in high school so I knew I wasn't ugly. Everyone had always said my dad was a looker and that I was the spitting image of him. Except he was straight as a string. I think he would've strangled me if he thought I liked dick. I wasn't about to tell him.

"It's not as big as your rod."

"Maybe you're still growing."

"Doubt that. It's been the same since I was thirteen."

"You're exactly what I like," he said. "I can't believe it. Muscular but natural bod. Dark good looks. Sultry. Bedroom eyes."

"So what do you want? Should I pay you for telling me I'm hot stuff? Sailors don't have money."

"I want your dick, kid. Want that big sucker up my ass. Want you to fuck me."

"Really?"

"Yo, hombre."

It was hard to believe. And I was kind of worried he might want to bury his big bone up *my* butt. No way I could have handled that.

I expected him to lie on his belly and I'd enter his backdoor. But no, he had other plans. With some maneuvering, I ended up lying on my back as he straddled me.

"I want to look at you when you fuck me," he said.

I was a fucking greenhorn and didn't know anything about position. But my cock was ready for action, stiff and drooling lube.

The blond lifted up and wet his crack with some spit. Then he sat right down on my hard cock. I didn't expect it to be that way. My cock slid right up his fiery, tight fuckhole. His butt-cheeks grazed my balls.

The blowjob had been incredible, but fucking ass was the real thing. He was so macho acting I hadn't imagined he'd want to be hit in the shitter — and by me! Well, life's full of surprises.

My hard dick was big enough to stretch an asshole and make it feel stuffed. The blond arched up and bounced his butt around on my cock. He reached down and pinched my tits. It felt like electricity coursing through my body. I didn't expect that sensation at all. I held onto his waist while he humped and hunched. I even began thrusting upwards into his butthole.

His cock was engorged while I pumped his hole. He took himself in hand and started beating his meat. I clutched his asscheeks and fucked that hot, smooth butt for all it was worth.

"Oh, it's so big," he moaned "So hard. I can feel it ready to shoot. Wait for me, motherfucker!"

His asshole clamped around my cock like a vise. Streams of his hot jizz spurted onto my chest. And I exploded inside him, tearing his ass up with my big cock.

"Aw fuck, it's never been like this," he gasped. "I think I'm in love."

I grinned back at him. He lifted up with a pained expression and got off my cock.

"Hungry for semen," he raved.

With his tongue he lapped up his own puddle of cum from my belly. He lay on top of me, pressed his lips against mine and trickled some of his salty jizz into my mouth.

I took another nip of the Jim Beam as a cum chaser.

"Thanks for the party," I said with a smile.

"You're special," he replied.

"Thanks." I was really glad he liked me.

Then he looked at me for a couple of moments before he spoke. "Two ships passing in the night . . ."

"Huh?"

"Nothing. Take an even strain, sailor."

I went back to my room to grab some z's. I'd rather have slept with the blond. I woke up with a boner and whacked off thinking about him.

The next day I took the bus to Treasure Island and reported for duty aboard the U.S.S. Interdiction, a small gray ship with a lot of radar equipment on it.

Going up the gangplank with my seabag, I stopped to salute the officer of the deck.

"Welcome aboard, sailor."

It couldn't be true. I was dreaming. The ensign who greeted me was my hunky blond. I later found out his name really was Jim Beam, like the whiskey. I think he was as shocked as I was, but he returned my salute. And there was no mistaking the gleam of delight in his eye.

LUCKY BAG

RICK JACKSON

I DON'T KNOW HOW to explain what first turned me on about Greg. It wasn't that he was super cute and built like a god. The ship had 500 other young, studly marines on it. As a typical sailor, I did a fair number of them at regular intervals, but none of them could make my guts churn by just walking into the room. Greg was more than just a fox with high cheekbones and a body like chiseled granite. He had a way of looking at you with omniscient grey eyes that made your spine turn to jelly and your flesh give a shiver.

When he spoke, you knew he was talking to *you* the way nobody else did. Something about his eyes and slightly crooked smile bored through the bullshit of everyday life aboard and found a secret, peaceful place that lurked deep within you, but which you yourself had never visited. He was open and sincere and completely artless in the way very small children are before they learn what life is really like and turn cynical.

Greg wasn't stupid, but he was centered and at home with himself, really more like a Zen master than a marine. When the rest of the company had their balls caught in a vise over some major clusterfuck or other, Greg would just smile at the irony of life. His detached, otherworldly approach would lay bare the absurdities of your problems and bring sunshine to your soul. One day about three months into the float, we were standing out on the weatherdecks out by Mount 31. I was going off about how my LPO was a dick — and, worse, a stupid, self-satisfied dick that got in the way of my doing my job. Nothing vexes me about the Nav more than the way some career pricks wear their smug ignorance like a badge of honor and keep it polished by constant use.

In a natural, completely unselfconscious gesture, Greg laid his right hand on my shoulder as his eyes locked onto mine and he said things would get better, eventually. At least, I assume that's what he said. The eyes and that goofy Tom Cruise grin were bad enough, but the feel of his strong hand at my shoulder and the soapy smell of his body just inches away from mine were too much. Once his hand touched my body, I didn't know anything except that I needed his tight gungy ass — yesterday.

His personality attracted me on one level, but my guts also knew every inch that he had to offer physically. When you spend months living on a ship with hundreds of marines, you know what they look like naked. Floating around in the Gulf summer of 135° in a 20-year-old ship designed by idiots, clothes are the last thing you need when you're in lounging around berthing. We shower naked. We sleep naked. We stroke around the compartment, watch TV, play cards, write letters home, and, if we are shy about using our shipmates, jack off naked.

Standing beside him with his hand on my shoulder, I couldn't hold back any longer. I stopped ranting about the gunny, looked through those grey eyes into his soul, and popped out despite myself, "Can I blow you?" For a minute, he just looked — trying to think. I might have used Hindi to ask about today's Dow Jones for all he comprehended. I could see the wheels turn, but he wasn't sure how to react.

Officially, sailors don't do marines; unofficially you'd be surprised what goes on during long floats — or ashore, for that matter. Most marines don't join the Corps because they crave camping out. I didn't know whether Greg was family or not, but just then I didn't give a shit. Gay or straight, I needed his dick. His mouth started to drop open so I tried again: "I want to suck your dick, to choke on your load, to give you head. I need bad what you need to blow."

He looked at me forever, then, in that easy-going way of his said, "Well, OK. If it will make you happy. Where?" Later I discovered that he hadn't been family — then. He'd been spanking the monkey a lot, but the idea of splashing a load down another tight marine hole hadn't occurred to him. I take back what I said before. Greg wasn't *exactly* stupid — slow maybe.

When I pulled his ass into a near-by fan room I'd used before doing other young desert defenders, he was obviously willing to humor me by going along with anything I wanted. If I needed a dick to suck, then he'd help me out. When I knelt before him and dropped his shorts, I saw I'd undervalued his charms. He was long and thick and, incredibly, just hanging there. The goof was practically virginal. Whenever some stud is about to chow down on my cream filling, I'm ramrod stiff and good to go.

I lapped at his ballbag and slipped my tongue up along his thigh to track down his day's crotch-sweat, but all he did was shiver. My worshipful hands eased along his flanks and up under his t-shirt, gliding across his soft, nearly hairless young marine body like a dragonfly across a mountain lake. As I buzzed here and there, seeking out his cobbled belly and tender tits, I slipped my lucky bag onto his pole. I call the rubber I always carry with me a lucky bag because it's there just in case Fortune throws something special my way. Besides, my lucky bags generally end up with filling any marine in his right mind would love to bid on.

Greg was no sooner condomized than my wet lips locked around the bottom of his shank and worked north to inhale the best eight inches of marine manhood a young lance corporal could want.

My hands instinctively slid around to his back. They worked by easy stages downward from his broad shoulders, across the small of his back, and locked by Nature onto Station Alpha: cupped around his huge, hard buttcheeks. As I polished his ass, I also pulled him tighter against me. His shank was halfway into my mouth by now and had finally started to swell and stiffen. His hips were rocking instinctively upward, driving his dick home, shoving his fat slab of marine meat down my throat as it swelled up and copped an attitude. My fingers couldn't believe the satin softness of his ass; my throat reveled in the pulsing strength of his long, thick tool.

I dropped his butt just long enough to kick off my UDTs. They'd long since popped open as my weasel wiggled free, expecting to join the action. I worked my lips around the base of his bone, snuggling tight into his dark blond bush and took an occasional slap at my own pressing business.

Once Greg's grunt lizard started to leap, he got with the program in one serious gungy way. Long before my tongue was finished playing with the throbbing blue vein that snaked along the length of his shod serpent, he was force-feeding me inch after inch of determined dick, driving it hard enough and far enough into my face that he actually found an inch or two of virgin throat.

By then, of course, I was grabbing ass more to keep him from face-fucking me to the deck than because I wanted to feel him up. Of course, I'd never have dreamed of gliding my hands down into his asscrack, stretching his hard mounds of marine manmuscle wide so I could put my finger right on love-pucker. If you believe that, you'd also believe I wouldn't come in your mouth. The question in this case was academic; the bastard was bashing away at my face so brutally, I had to do something to hold on. Well, maybe once I was in the neighborhood anyway, I did jam my fuckfinger inside his shithole, but only to the first knuckle. The way his hips took off once I was up his ass told me he didn't object.

Only when he was slamming his blond pubes hard enough into my face to risk whiplash did I realize I'd only brought one rubber. As he was fucking my throat and I was feeling around up inside his ass, one small, very remote corner of my mind wrestled with an ethical conundrum. Marines are HIV-tested regularly. He was almost certainly safe as an ugly spinster. I was 99.9% sure I was clear; my last test had only been 2 months before. On the other hand, I knew deep down that much as I wanted my stiff dick up his ass, I wasn't going to risk present danger and the future agonies of uncertainty just to hone a heavenly bone now. I'd put off until tomorrow what I could do today. I did think in passing about unrolling the rubber from his rod and sliding it, inside out down my own, but I could already feel its insides awash with pre-cum. The only option left was for the marine-hungry dick to use the rubber on me.

I'm a top, but something about Greg was such a massive, gloriously perverted turn-on, the idea of being done hard up the ass by the thick eight inches down my throat didn't do anything but get me harder. I felt Greg's ballbag contract, pounding now against my chin. If I was going to give up the ultimate in marine fox holes, I knew I had to do it soon, before Greg was satisfied and of no further immediate use to either of us.

I hooked my finger hard inside Greg's tight marine butt and used it and my free hand to pry his hips away from my mouth. After doing me the favor of face-fucking me, Greg didn't think I was showing proper appreciation when I let his swollen and very lonely need slap up against his bare belly. I said we needed to wait, but the slut would have bitched if I hadn't been lapping my way up past his belly button to gnaw on his hairless tits. To really titillate him, I had to unplug his hole and use both hands to slip his t-shirt over his head. I thought about leaving it over his face or, churlishly, of using it as a gag to stifle his moans and grunts of pleasure as I slid the dangerous edges of my teeth along his tits. I hoped the AC fans roaring away behind us were making enough to drown out our noise, but just then I was having so much fun I doubt either of us was thinking straight. It's a wonder we were even able to think gay.

When his tits were tamed and tenderized, I slipped up to lick his armpits free of their musky man-scent and angled on up to give his ear the best tongue-lashing any young grunt could want. My hands had long since slid over every shuddering cobble on the muscular road to masculine perfection he thought of as government property. His flanks and broad shoulders, his butt and the track of his spine all fell victim to my rabid, rapine touch, shivering and shuddering as I passed across his flesh and inflated my own bone even more.

Squeezing and tugging at his heavy balls like any experienced critic of stallion flesh, my hands promised me Greg's tool could stand some more time tangling with my tonsils without blowing a good thing down my gullet. I was licking my way back down to his log when I changed my mind. If I really was going to make him the first man up my ass in ages, postponing his fucking pleasure wouldn't do either of us any good. I thought about making him beg for it, but I knew he'd be sniffing around plenty from now on. The next time we did the bone dance, I'd have a half dozen rubbers handy and flood them all.

Greg may not have been a typical marine buttfucker, but when I turned tail on him and braced myself against the bulkhead, he didn't need any pictures drawn. He hadn't done much except lock his hands around my head while he was conducting my tonsil exam; but now that he was in the driver's seat, he used them plenty. They were tentative at first, unfamiliar with the feel of another man's ready body. As they slid across the strange country of my man's muscle, they learned the ancient need of our military brotherhood and the confidence to meat it.

His lips brushed against the nape of my neck, his hot, tortured, bestial breath roared in my ears. Fingers tore at my tits and ruffled away at the wiry red hair that lives across my pecs and belly. His body snuggled spoon-like against me, slipping my bare back through a layer of our shared sweat and hard against his hairless chest and belly. His hips ground against my ass, working his meat between my clenching mounds of firm manmuscle. Greg may have been a boot, but his dick knew as much as a sergeant fucking major. It knew how to use my ass-sweat to slide along my valley of delight. It knew how to use my cheeks to jerk himself off as they reflexively wrapped around his rod. It especially knew where to find my asshole.

Greg's hand slid down to my hips to pull my pelvis tight against his warrior's tool. Neither the snarl in his breath or the roll of his lips left much doubt Greg had learned what he wanted — or that I was about to be his devil-dog bitch of a sea-pussy. Even with my hands wrapped hard around a pipe and my teeth clenched, when it came, the pain was as unimaginable as it was indescribable. I'd sucked Greg's swell to a swollen, but his own passion had long since pumped his proud peter to a perfect pounder that needed nothing so much as to bray my butt to shreds.

No particle of his former understanding remained alive in him. He rammed his rod into me, battering open the gates of my long-surrendered virtue. Wave after soul-blinding wave of gut-wrenching agony roared up from my ass to reverberate like the Klaxon of Doom about my consciousness. I cranked my shank to keep up with him and, I hoped, help keep my mind off the torment. His rubbered rod was too dry and, delightfully worse, too thick for me to take lying down — or standing up or hanging from the overhead. But take it I did. Somehow. His impossible marine weapon ripped cruelly in and out of my guts as they clenched tight against the shock of sublime violation. Somehow, though, the clenching helped slather my ass-juices along his log and trans-mute the terrible pain of his dick up my ass into an even more awful, immaculate, and ineffable ecstasy. That rhapsody swept across my consciousness, numbing my mind as it numbed my butt to take the punishment that was coming. In a last glimmer of consciousness and caution, I slipped my jack-hand back to grip his shank for a moment to be sure the rubber was in better shape than my ass. It had held firm, but the animal instinct ruling

Greg's rape of my ass saw the hand between us as a threat and switched his frenzied dick into overdrive to teach me the lesson we both already knew.

I grabbed my joint and held on tight, grinding my butt along his dick when I could, trying to keep from screaming out in painful pleasure when I remembered where we were, determined to stay conscious throughout so I would remember everything: the feel of our sweat splashing between us, the way Greg's rod rammed my guts out of its way only to leave a terrible vacuum inside me a moment later, his hands clawing at my hips and chest and shoulders, the loud, sloppy thwack of muscle against flesh, his moans and jarhead grunts and muffled screams filling my ears with his terrible torment, and most of all, the soul-numbing satisfaction of giving myself so completely to someone I respected and admired and, perhaps, even loved?

By the time Greg's hands clutched at my chest thatch, his breath grew as selfish and savage as his dick, and his hips ran amok to pump my lucky bag full of his frothy marine load. As I shot my own load up against the bulkhead, I was sure that the eternity of those finite minutes Greg used me as his bitch had changed me forever as completely as they had changed him. Even after my butt eventually recovered from the damage that thick, gloriously impetuous animal dick had done up my ass, I would remember the lesson it had drilled into me. His bone may not have trained me to be a bottom, but it taught me to recognize a good thing in the right place. I may not have turned Greg entirely away from women, but he sure as shit knew what to do with a buddy on a float.

Later that day I salvaged enough strength to find Greg for a rematch — armed this time with a whole pocketful of protection. My ass remembered him and welcomed him home; but when he was finished, I made good my promise to show him how a real military man can meat his objective — inside the Corps or out. In the end, Greg was stoically coöperative, but, even afterwards, he obstinately claimed he perferred being a top, too. I'm sure eventually I'll be able to teach his ass where it belongs: wrapped around my swollen pole. Meanwhile, I guess we'll just have to keep training Greg until he gets it right.

A Grunt Glossary

Boot — what the Navy calls a "bootcamp"; a green unit, a military man so new (just out of boot camp) he doesn't know the score, a naïf, a fucking cherry.

ClusterFuck — What a grain of sand is to a desert or a tree is to a forest, a clusterfuck is to a fuck-up; military life; anything the military tries to do; an over-produced, underdirected, mismanaged SNAFU of epic scale.

Devil-dogs — since WWI, a term used for marines (originally by Germans), leathernecks, jarheads, the finest fuck any young man could find.

Fan room — a closet-sized space on Navy ships where AC equipment is housed and privacy is usually available.

Gungy — from "gung-ho." Dedicated, determined, loyal to the Corps and always eager to serve. The attitude the Corps likes to see in its men.

Gunny — See "Squad Leader."

Lucky bag — as normally used, a bag or box into which "gear adrift" (unauthorized items like CD players, shoes, sunglasses, etc. found in and confiscated from crew berthing) is placed until it can be auctioned off to the highest bidder.

Mount 31 — one of the two 5-inch gun mounts on a certain class of Navy ship (LSTs) that carries marines; the only weapon on a ship bigger than those swinging between marine thighs — or that goes off with a bigger bang.

Squad leader — the only known creature that is at once a dick *and* an asshole, yet has no redeeming value.

UDTs — [Underwater Diving Trunks] khaki shorts with an easy-to-open belt and easier-to-open button fly. So short they may hide some dicks but few marine butts; the best uniform item afloat mainly because most men don't wear briefs; balls and the occasional dick *will* wander out, especially when the wearer is seated. The shorts are worn by embarked marines in the Gulf and some naval personnel, who don't look nearly as good in them (or out of them) as the United States Marines.

Weatherdecks — The exterior decks of a ship; at night, a place where marines could be alone together with the starlight if only Navy personnel would stay inside where they belong.

BOOKS FROM LEYLAND PUBLICATIONS/G.S. PRESS

AIDS RISK REDUCTION GUIDELINES
FOR HEALTHIER SEX

As given by Bay Area Physicians for Human Rights

NO RISK: *Most of these activities involve only skin-to-skin contact, thereby avoiding exposure to blood, semen, and vaginal secretions. This assumes there are no breaks in the skin.* 1) **Social kissing** (dry). 2) **Body massage, hugging.** 3) **Body to body rubbing** (frottage). 4) **Light S&M** (without bruising or bleeding). 5) **Using one's own sex toys.** 6) **Mutual masturbation** (male or external female). Care should be taken to avoid exposing the partners to ejaculate or vaginal secretions. Seminal, vaginal and salivary fluids should not be used as lubricants.

LOW RISK: *In these activities small amounts of certain body fluids might be exchanged, or the protective barrier might break causing some risk.* 1) **Anal or vaginal intercourse with condom.** Studies have shown that HIV does not penetrate the condom in simulated intercourse. Risk is incurred if the condom breaks or if semen spills into the rectum or vagina. The risk is further reduced if one withdraws before climax. 2) **Fellatio interruptus** (sucking, stopping before climax). Pre-ejaculate fluid may contain HIV. Saliva or other natural protective barriers in the mouth may inactivate virus in pre-ejaculate fluid. Saliva may contain HIV in low concentration. The insertive partner should warn the receptive partner before climax to prevent exposure to a large volume of semen. If mouth or genital sores are present, risk is increased. Likewise, action which causes mouth or genital injury will increase risk. 3) **Fellatio with condom** (sucking with condom) Since HIV cannot penetrate an intact condom, risk in this practice is very low unless breakage occurs. 4) **Mouth-to-mouth kissing** (French kissing, wet kissing) Studies have shown that HIV is present in saliva in such low concentration that salivary exchange is unlikely to transmit the virus. Risk is increased if sores in the mouth or bleeding gums are present. 5) **Oral-vaginal or oral-anal contact with protective barrier.** e.g. a latex dam, obtainable through a local dental supply house, may be used. Do not reuse latex barrier, because sides of the barrier may be reversed inadvertently. 6) **Manual anal contact with glove** (manual anal (fisting) or manual vaginal (internal) contact with glove). If the glove does not break, virus transmission should not occur. However, significant trauma can still be inflicted on the rectal tissues leading to other medical problems, such as hemorrhage or bowel perforation. 7) **Manual vaginal contact with glove** (internal). See above.

MODERATE RISK: *These activities involve tissue trauma and/or exchange of body fluids which may transmit HIV or other sexually transmitted disease.* 1) **Fellatio** (sucking to climax). Semen may contain high concentrations of HIV and if absorbed through open sores in the mouth or digestive tract could pose risk. 2) **Oral-anal contact** (rimming). HIV may be contained in blood-contaminated feces or in the anal rectal lining. This practice also poses high risk of transmission of parasites and other gastrointestinal infections. 3) **Cunnilingus** (oral-vaginal contact). Vaginal secretions and menstrual blood have been shown to harbor HIV, thereby causing risk to the oral partner if open lesions are present in the mouth or digestive tract. 4) **Manual rectal contact** (fisting). Studies have indicated a direct association between fisting and HIV infection for both partners. This association may be due to concurrent use of recreational drugs, bleeding, pre-fisting semen exposure, or anal intercourse with ejaculation. 5) **Sharing sex toys.** 6) **Ingestion of urine.** HIV has not been shown to be transmitted via urine; however, other immunosuppressive agents or infections may be transmitted in this manner.

HIGH RISK: *These activities have been shown to transmit HIV.* 1) **Receptive anal intercourse without condom.** All studies imply that this activity carries the highest risk of transmitting HIV. The rectal lining is thinner than that of the vagina or the mouth thereby permitting ready absorption of virus from semem or pre-ejaculate fluid to the blood stream. One laboratory study suggests that the virus may enter by direct contact with rectal lining cells without any bleeding. 2) **Insertive anal intercourse without condom.** Studies suggest that men who participate only in this activity are at less risk of being infected than their partners who are rectally receptive; however, the risk is still significant. It carries high risk of infection by other sexually transmitted diseases. 3) **Vaginal intercourse without condom.**